The Land of Nod

Jonathan Gabel

For Miranda. My love and my life. My light and my darkness.

You make the hell that created this book feel like paradise.

"Happiness must be, for most men and women, an achievement rather than a gift of the gods."

-Bertrand Russel.

CONTENTS

1 | Gotta Get My Mind Right

A God died today.

I can feel the asphalt grind my nostrils as the steam lifts it from the street below. It's a record high today and I'm basically swimming in my suit. I keep removing the folded stack of bills from my jacket pocket, counting it religiously, and then placing it back. It counts the same every time, and devious thoughts of flesh and fantasy fill my troubled mind as I pass the strung out junkies who are up like clockwork scheming for their daily high. Eight months off the shit and seeing their pain and panic every morning still causes my mouth to salivate. I'm making decent scratch now, doing daily pick-ups and odd jobs for Lou, but the insanity of it all is that more days than not, I walk home desiring nothing more than to trade realities with those bums nodding out in the alley. I feel like I've been content in a purgatory of ambivalence for months now, unsure whether to drop back down to hell or reach for heaven.

Last pickup of the day is at Pauly's joint. The locals call it the Temple of Fuck. In the seventies and eighties it was one of the biggest porn studios in the city. That all changed once the AIDS and coke epidemics ate through most of their workers. Pauly ended up buying it off the studios for cheap and turned it into what some call "the playground" for the sexually and morally depraved.

The sin has a tendency to hit you right in the back of the throat every time you swing open that heavy wooden door and walk in the place. If it wasn't for the huge chunk of Lou's revenue originating here I'd never step foot inside. I dig the joint a little too much, but today I have personal business to attend to.

This city is rife with addiction. My veteran eyes grow more keen to its sick signature with every passing day, and there is no better example of its pen stroke than The Temple of Fuck. As I walk in, I spot Frank serving three barflies who seem to grow out of the bar like a fungus; mucus membranes sucking straws like a sole source of sustenance. The lights are overly dim as always and an uncomfortable sense of shame hangs in the shadows.

"Jesus Christ Frank, don't you ever fucking mop this place?" I say with a playful disdain.

2

Frank has tended bar there for as long as I can remember. He chokes back the rest of his bourbon before turning to respond.

"Not my department, Rick. You know that."

"Well you should really hire someone to get on it. I can feel the cum gluing my shoes to the floor"

"You know for a low life you sure are one high strung mother fucker"

"Oh, I forgot not wanting a hundred pervert's jizz slathered on my new Cole Haans was a staple of the aristocracy. Thanks for the heads-up. And cool it with the junkie talk."

"You and I both know that becoming a junkie is a one way ticket Rick, you may be off the shit for now, but you and I both know it still courses through your veins." Frank scoffs.

"Frank, you'd be wise to learn that all men are broken, the only difference is to what degree."

Part of me knows I am writing off his comment with philosophical poppycock, and a large part of me agrees with him. Well aware of my desires day in and day out, how could I not? I decide not to argue any further.

"Is Pauly in?"

"Yeah, he's upstairs. Door should be open. Don't be a stranger Rick."

"Frank... you know damn well that Lou would never do something as nice as allow me to leave and never step foot in this pit again," I say as I head towards the staircase in the corner.

The wooden steps whine as I march upwards. The sudden striking emergence of light as I round the corner throws me off-center. I pause mid-step as my senses cause a retreat into the past. Mia floods my mind. I am stuck in a loop of revelry as I imagine her legs tight around my face, my lungs barely escaping asphyxiation. My stream of consciousness quickly flows to the blissful times; the untouched comfort of her asleep in my arms, her warm pale skin glimmering in the morning sun like a lost jewel. Memories that still prick my mind like an untreated wound. Through my countless spiritual searches, these are truly the only times in my life I've felt anything near the universal unification the Buddhists profess. My step falters and I catch myself as reality returns to the forefront of my perception. I'm still not sure if my nightly insomnia, and the resulting fog that drifts through my mind on a daily basis stems from grieving the boy or the girl. The two now seem paradoxically intertwined, heroin and honey.

The light is a stale yellow that skitters down the steps, not exactly behaving like light at all. The intermittent pulsation of which fosters a dull ache in my temple. I walk in to find Pauly sitting behind his desk, king over his kingdom. His glazed eyes pass over a pile of Polaroid's featuring girls who should be planning their sweet sixteen, but instead look ahead with a soulless dead gaze.

"Catch of the day?"

Pauly somehow pulls off glaring at me and shooting me a perverted smile simultaneously.

"Rick fucking Thompson, I didn't know it was Thursday already," he says, ignoring the snipe.

"Lou didn't send me."

"I'm intrigued. I'll pour you a rum, then? Since this isn't business."

"I mean, I'll grab the money while I'm here, but no, this isn't business. Rum will be fine."

"Fantastic," Pauly says as he grabs a couple glasses and starts to pour. "You know, you joke about my girls, but Talent is the future my friend. Nobody wants to be rich anymore. Fame is the new currency of the people. There are three types in this world, Rick: Those who are rich, those who are poor, and those who are famous. And the rich are just poor people with money."

"Interesting life philosophy you got there, Pauly. Let me know when they get to their drugged-up, dark girl phase, and maybe I can help you out."

Pauly expels a quick burst of laughter, speaking without the slightest hint of patience to catch his breath.

"That's fucking funny. You will be first on my call list, Rick."

I lift a small smirk of acknowledgement for Pauly's compliment. I care very little for his petty acceptance, but I can tell he senses my apathy for the conversation at hand. I take a sip of the rum to ease the moment.

"Damn, you are breaking out the good shit today, Pauly. Columbian, isn't it? I can taste the wood off the nose."

"Yeah, yeah, it's Columbian," Pauly said as any facade of levity and patience drains from his face. "Cut the shit, Rick. You didn't come here for business. You didn't come here to talk about my girls or my rum. And I know damn well after that night two years ago, you'd never come here for pleasure. So why don't you explain why the fuck are you in my office, drinking my rum, and talking about my girls."

"Geez, Pauly, so much for the pleasantries."

"You don't think I know why you are here? You think I'm going to believe its just a coincidence that the day I get this shipment in, you show up out of the blue?"

"Shipment?"

"Get the fuck out of my office you little prick. I'm done playing your games, and you better hope I'm in a better mood the next time I talk to Lou. Cause I'm not one to fuck around with this kind of shit."

"Pauly, come on, it's me. Alright, I know about the shipment." I hope my bluff will quell his anger. "I was hoping I could pick one up off you. I've got the cash."

"You kidding me Rick? The Meiser group would have my head, and then fuck it, if I let one of these go early. I appreciate your dedication to the game kid, but you are in over your head here."

"Can I at least see what you're working with?"

"Do you promise to get the fuck outta here and forget about this shit if I indulge your junkie fantasies?"

"That sounds fair." We both know I'll never see this agreement through, but Pauly clearly just wants to do whatever will get me to leave without issue.

He turns to the painting behind his desk and begins to enter the combination to the safe in the wall behind it. The cliché nature of this scene always slaps me with a sense of surrealism. As he counts the money owed, my eyes tense up, focused on a box pushed to the back of the safe. Dread permeates my nature.

"Pauly, what do you know about the Meiser Group? Is it true they have found a cure for junk sickness?"

The question sobers his demeanor.

He reluctantly removes the box, as if he feels the safe is protecting him from it more than the safe is protecting it from the outside world. The box looks to be composed of muscle and bound by sinew, and gives the appearance of reacting to his touch. Out of instinct, I strain to check my hands--am I hallucinating? As he places the box on the table, it seems to breathe with me in tandem. He props open the lid to reveal four syringes seemingly constructed out of bone and cartilage, each one looking at home in their notches. Two slots lay bare; this perversion appears to me as if a smile lacking a tooth.

I blink and catch myself choking on a drag of cigarette I don't remember taking. I'm outside my apartment in the boroughs and night has fallen. Rain pours so heavy my eyes are hypnotically drawn to the pavement much like to the analog static of a television. Solid neon lights in the distance are cut into waves and the smoke from my cigarette can't make it a foot without its graceful flow being dissipated by the downpour.

I walk upstairs and try to make sense of what happened earlier, grasping at air, trying to fill the lost time in my head. This would be about the time I'd usually pump my blood full of cocaine to remember, to push forward, or shoot some heroin to forget anything happened at all. But not tonight.

While passing the coffee table, I acknowledge and then forcefully ignore the pile of bills that grows bigger with each passing day. Noodling on the keys for a while helps my mind retreat from words; so much of my mind is comprised of words and ideas and, god, more words.

I call up an old lover and we pretend to be into each other for a little while. I ask her to come over and she once again tells me her boyfriend will be coming over tonight.

"All your boyfriend ever does is interfere with my coke binges."

"I know... Same."

I finally understand the meaning of down and out. I hadn't had a writing gig in months. I daily tried to represent a sort of neo-beatnik, wanting to bring an intellectualism back to junkiedom. Eradicate once and for all this faux intellectualism that seems to have infected the left.

Rawness, Feeling, Emotion, and Passion all for once in balance with reason and an intellectual witticism.

Yet, without the drugs, I feel alienated from the very thing I wish to express, and while on them, I find my other passions don't get much attention, if any all.

I'm drawn into my bathroom and I start the shower. The head hisses as steam escapes from its beady holes. I shed my clothes onto the bathroom floor but the stresses of the day seem deeply imbedded in my skin. My nightly meditation has become my only respite from the daily madness of this city. I lay my bones down into the basin of the shower and the searing pain of the water striking my chest blocks out the world around me. The cool blue light of the moon slices through the calescent fog, a fog that causes the fleshy tissue of my lungs to sweat with each inhalation. I sit in silence, attempting to batter away past memories and future anxieties to no avail. I ruminate over what's driving me, why I continue to perpetuate this suffering day after day, constantly fighting off my natural instinct to do nothing? And why, despite this feeling in my gut, I push myself forward with a complete absence of pay off? I feel no love or hate, just time, stretching out endlessly, and I float along, numb and empty.

I snap out of my meditation as a series of knocks echoes into my consciousness. The shit wasn't helping anyways. I jump out of the shower and throw on a well-worn robe as the knocks increase in frequency and urgency.

Against the drab brown peeling wallpaper and piss yellow light of the hallway is projected a vision. There stands Mia, barely holding up the weight of her own body, hair dripping wet like chocolate with streaks of warm honey. My pride kicks up as an immediate reaction to the sting of the past, but my resolve quickly dissolves the longer I stare into those defeated hazel eyes. I'm unsure if her mascara stained cheeks are a result of the rain or her tears. A word isn't spoken, she just lets go and falls into my arms, saying all she has to with her eyes. I'd follow those eyes into the gates of hell. She moves to kiss me and as her lips dance with mine the past is made white as snow.

"I fucking missed you babe" I say with sheer joy and rapidity.

"I missed you, too."

Her smile tells me everything is going to be alright, despite all past evidence to the contrary, and I believe it. Mia and I have a history, a history much like that of the Roman empire. The highs were high, and it couldn't have gotten much lower. But despite all that, my soul always carried a special weakness for Mia, and my awareness of that weakness never made much of a difference.

"Why don't you grab a seat on the couch and we can talk about the sudden re-emergence of Mia Vaughn. Rum alright?"

"Yeah, cut it with coke, will ya?"

I walk into the kitchen, fill two glasses with spiced rum on ice, pour coke into hers, and grab a marble ashtray from the cabinet. As I make my way into the common room with the drinks, I notice something strange on the coffee table wrapped in white linen. I flick a couple of cigarettes out of my pack and offer Mia one, preparing myself for what's to come. I light the smoke dangling from Mia's lips and then proceed to light my own. The smoke is warm and smooth like caramel. It pacifies me only for a moment until she out and says it.

"Where are your works?"

Any sense of calm that may have resided in my mind due to her presence quickly drains as the beast in the back of my mind ferociously awakens due to those four little words. I've grown strong in eight months and at first I quickly shut the thoughts down.

"Sorry, babe," I hesitate, wary of her reaction. "I know it's been a while -a long while- but I'm off the junk, have been for almost a year now"

She doesn't seem to hesitate at all; in fact, she shows no emotional response to my news.

"Just go grab me something to tie off with. You don't have to do any if you don't want."

The words reverberate in my head. I don't have to do any... If I don't want... The choice is now quite literally on the table, and the beast inside my brain responds instantly to the blood in the water. I walk into my bedroom and pick up the first belt I had ever tied off with; even after all these years, I hadn't gotten rid of it. I find a junkie shares a special bond with his belt, an unbreakable soul tie that isn't severed even after long periods of not using. My veins have already risen to the surface on both arms, seemingly sentient and conscious of the decision I'll make before my mind is. They are begging to be fed.

I re-enter the common room and before I can even turn the corner a sense of tension settles on my body. The linen is now open on the table and in it is unmistakably one of the bone syringes I saw at Pauly's earlier.

"Where did you get that?" I snap, struck paranoid by the coincidence.

"It doesn't matter. Do you want in on this or what?"

12

"Fuck all it doesn't matter. You know the kind of shit I almost got into this afternoon with Pauly over one of those things? I swear to god, the box it was in looked like it was fucking alive. It might have been for all I know. I've been trying to forget that box all night, and here you come, back into my life out of nowhere, and you just happen to have one of those...things. I'm just supposed to ignore that and not find this all a bit too strange?"

"Well, you know our relationship with fate, Rick."

"Alright... You wouldn't be saying that if you saw what I saw." I laugh nervously.

"I saw the box. Where else do you think I got this? They aren't exactly selling these at the corner store."

"And you took it anyway? Jesus, what have I done to you?"

"Yeah, it's always about you, Lord Rick shepherding all of us sheep off the cliff of life."

"Okay, well..." I pause hoping she gets the hint. "You gotta tell me the story. How did you pull this off? I tried to hand Pauly a wad of cash this afternoon and almost lost my job."

"Well, I'll have you know, there is a perfectly sane explanation. Last night, I was on day three of an awesome bender, and I ended up at The Temple of Fuck, as people tend to do on day three of a bender. Money had dried up, I was sick, so I went up to Pauly's office to see if I could work something out..."

"Jesus, Mia..."

"Fuck off. Why do you always have to assume I'm whoring myself out? Listen, I went up to Pauly's office and he was drunker than usual, nearly comatose. His safe was wide open. At this point, I was so dope sick, I figured this was a fucking miracle. So I crept behind Pauly and checked the safe for the dope he usually keeps in there or at the very least some cash..."

"And...?"

"Yeah... Despite all the shit I'm giving you, you are not wrong. That feeling of fortune passed pretty damn quickly the moment I saw that box. But I was sick and desperate, so I cracked it open and snatched two hoping I could pawn them off to someone at the very least."

"Shit, you've done one of these already?"

I consider what this might mean. Could she be cured?

"Have you been dope sick since then?" I ask.

"Nah, I couldn't do it. Believe me I tried. Every time I'd put the needle anywhere near my arm I'd start trembling. That's not like me; I love needles, you know that. So I ended up trading one of them for enough boy to get me straight 'til today, but I just couldn't let the other one go."

"Only you would trade a Picasso for a Thomas Kinkade, just because the Picasso didn't quite make you feel warm inside. I hope the high was worth it. You know word on the street is those things cure The Sickness right?"

"You gotta be kidding me! Seriously?"

"Yeah, but I don't buy it. I've been trying to figure out more since I first heard about it, but it's just dead end after dead end. Today with Pauly was the closest I've got. My theory is this Meiser Group, whoever they are, want some level of control over the junkies of this city, but for what?"

Mia rolls her eyes.

"Well, I was hoping you would want to do it with me. I thought you would get a kick out of it. You've done more drugs then there are names for."

"Not yet, not today"

"For Christ's sake, Rick, if I'd've known you were going to be such a pussy about this, I would have taken this shit elsewhere."

She strokes my ego and belittles me simultaneously, and combined with the hostility in our discourse, this creates the perfect cocktail to push the brimming sexual tension between us over the edge. My cheek twitches as I force down the last of my now-watered-down rum. I take the final drag of my cigarette, look at Mia with a glimmer in my eye, and extinguish the butt.

"Well, if we are going to do this, we might as well do this right."

A smile beams from her face, and just like that, I am back in her good graces. I don't kid myself; she always knew I was hers body and soul.

2 | God's Dumpster

It was eight years prior; the night still rings heavy in my memory. I was painting the town to commemorate twenty summers on a planet that still didn't quite feel like home, surprised my body was still taking orders from my mind after dosing the 450mg of powder dxm I had extracted earlier. I had made my way to Johnny's pad to score some boy to ease myself down and end the night right. Most normal human beings would consider his place a hellhole, the carpet probably hadn't been vacuumed in over a year, and I wouldn't have been surprised if he had gotten his shit-brown couches off the street, but home is where the H is. Setting never matters much to a junkie; I could be content fixing up under a bridge, as long as the dope was good. His place was The Plaza Hotel as far as I was concerned.

Johnny sat in the living room, the lumps of his body and the lumps of the couch indistinguishable, his hands so engorged they seemed as if they would pop with next needle he stuck in. He had the slumped back

17

of a man too tired to do anything else, always puffing on his cigarette as if it had an expiration date.

He was an old dead head with the demeanor of a bulldog, and way too much energy for a junkie. The junk had pushed him too far; it was a gut reaction to want to look away every time you saw the scars on his arms that would make a burn victim look pretty. But he exuded a charisma that drew you in, despite the innate sense that everything he said in the present was bullshit. Johnny was a denizen of the past and a delusional future; he could tell stories for days that would inspire an unthinkable amount of empathy for the moment in question. You felt you were there consciously and emotionally. He never stressed about what was to come, despite all the historic evidence to the contrary. I've found that junkies are the most delusionally optimistic people you will ever meet, always thinking that big score is right around the corner.

As I sat, I saw that he already had a birthday shot prepped and ready to go. Free heroin should never sour one's mood, but I remember getting a little pissed off because half the fun of heroin is in the ritual.

I remember Black by Pearl Jam was peaking as I registered and pushed in the plunger.

The music's effort was to pull me deeper, but the pains from the past this line pricked snapped me out of the slight rush and into a sudden state of lucidity.

18

"God dammit, Johnny, can we change the music? And throw me another bag, I'm not feeling this shit."

I glare in Johnny's direction and he returns the favor. Both of us knowing he had purposefully made the shot weak. Johnny is notorious for shorting and keeping some for himself. I throw a ten on the table in Johnny's general direction, grab another bag, and squirt the blood from my rig onto the wall behind us. The blood splatters that have accumulated on the wall can only be described as looking like some kind of fucked up junkie Jackson Pollack.

"What? You got a problem with Vedder?" He cocks up and it's clear this isn't about the music; more so that the man's ego can't handle being called out.

"Come on man, you know I can dig on some Pearl Jam. Shit's just bringing me down. Can't you just do me a solid and put on some Talking Heads or something with a little funk behind it?"

On any other day Johnny's pride would have locked him in place, but he obliges my request due to the celebration at hand.

I bob my head as David Byrne chants and wails under the interference of Johnny's subpar stereo set. I take my kit out of my bag and prepare for sacrament. My kit is an old wooden box, short and rectangular. I open the lid and place each relic, one by one, before me on the table. First my spoon; the holy chalice, then an unopened needle; my flaming sword, some fresh cotton; the purificator, and

19

finally some water blessed by yours truly. Once the ingredients are mixed and filtered I put flame to the spoon...

"And the smoke of the incense, with the prayers of the saints, went up before God out of the angel's hand."

"God dammit Rick, can you cool it with the blasphemy?"

Johnny is awfully spiritual for a man who clearly states there is no God with every action he takes, but not wanting to create any more conflict I shut my mouth. Cow flesh drips with saliva; my mouth knows what is to come and grips the bitter leather belt tightly. I quickly find a vein and complete my blood sacrifice. The star of the morning has risen.

Junk shows a man complete solitude and with it comes a true realization of solipsism. This is why most junkies become more and more isolated over time. Their soul withers away without the sunlight of communion so needed by every man.

As the junk rises up my spine, my eyes fall heavy and the music cries faint in the distance. The void welcomes me, unbidden. Its isolation from the harsh realities of the world bring every atom in my mind to a place of total and utter contentment. I retreat to the recesses of my mind, my inner sanctum. My flesh sizzles and evaporates, and ceases to be of any concern to me. I am, at this very moment, the one true god of my reality, and I create it as I see fit, and it is good. The reverie I find myself in allows me to fill in the recesses of my mind. I lay in awe beneath a single oak tree, no ground beneath, and the sky is dark and filled with static.

The rush of the heroin passes and I get up and make my way outside to smoke a cigarette. The cigarette fades in the blink of an eye, as nothing seems to concern me anymore, not even the simple pleasures. As I walk back inside I see that we are no longer alone. Johnny is finishing up a deal with a girl who looks way too young to be fucking with anything Johnny is selling. But just like that the night gets more interesting.

Torn jeans barely cling to her tiny waist and a tattered, plaid button down tell me that she's trying awfully hard to hide her striking natural beauty, but it isn't working. She pours her bag of H onto a pocket mirror, cuts it into lines, and snorts one before even acknowledging my existence.

I lean in close to Johnny's ear and try to subtlety inquire about her situation, hoping the distance between couches and the hit of heroin she just took to the brain is enough to keep her from noticing. He informs me that she is fifteen. The number stings to ears, but my flesh perks up at the sound.

Fifteen... I didn't believe it; she has the body of a sixteen year old at least.

I ask him to introduce me and he looks at me with both judgment and warning, but proceeds.

"Hey girl, don't mean to kill your buzz, but I have someone you gotta meet."

She slowly opens her eyes and uses what looks to be all her effort just to take in the world around her.

"This is my friend Rick, Rick this is Mia."

I extend my hand to greet her, but she quickly recedes into the couch with little more than an upward nod. To her credit, the junk was damn good.

And just like that, my contentment grows dim; an apparition of eloquence enters, ringing in the dawn of a new day, haunting the recesses of my arrantly desolate soul. I start prepping another shot, this time with a little coke as a sort of peacocking maneuver, hoping my energy and charisma will elicit some sort of response in the girl. My spirit sails, longing for a body to inhabit, a body to call home. My now abdicated exoskeleton no longer satisfies.

3 | Baby I Need Your Loving

Dawn breaks and no dice. I walk the apathetic streets with no particular destination, shattered and empty, knowing things will never be the same. The air is crisp and the palm trees flicker in the warm glow of the morning sun, but the beauty of the world is dulled by this realization that I can't sit in my own skin, the realization that without Mia, life is meaningless. I ruminate over courses of action in my head. My only connection to the girl is through Johnny. I haven't a clue where she lives or hangs out, nor did I pull off getting her digits.

After blowing my life savings last night celebrating, shooting H at Johnny's pad 'til she shows back up isn't really an option. I pull a joint out of my pocket, light it, and choke the smoke back, hoping for a little inspiration. I walk past Frankie's Diner and spot my car in the same space I left it in a few days prior. A bite doesn't sound like a bad idea, given that the last meal I had was two days ago when I left the car here in the first place.

Frankie's is one of those classic joints. I doubt the building has been touched beyond minor repairs since the late fifties. The dull chrome and burnt out neon lights are a pretty poetic representation of the clientele that call this place home.

This early in the morning, the stools are usually filled with drunks, either still blotto or wishing they were. Those no longer drunk were rapidly trying to clog their arteries in an attempt to stop any more blood from cleansing their alcohol soaked brains.

Then, of course, you have the Tweakers. Somehow both crusty and dripping with sweat, always appearing as if their body couldn't handle itself anymore. Usually, you will find them chatting it up in the corner at a table devoid of any food. They are easily contenders for my least favorite people on this god forsaken planet. Empty babbling pouring forth from their mouths, and more energy than anyone wants to deal with at this hour of the morning. I have yet to figure out why they even hang out here, as I can't recall a single instance of them ordering anything.

Lastly you have the Junkies, who are only up this early if they have come down with the sickness. They sit slouched, barely sipping on coffee, consistently phasing between complete lethargy and bursts of excitement at any cockeyed scheme that might result in a score; like an old dog who is only roused to excitement once a day when the mailman drops by. Probably the saddest sight in the joint, but it doesn't make them feel any less like family. I thank junkie Jesus every day that I have not caught the sickness yet, and sadly, somehow, seeing firsthand how it infects those around me doesn't even slow my descent into madness. I know it's inevitable; I know after a year and some change on the shit, it's gotta be right around the corner, and I fear all I can do is watch, paralyzed, as it happens.

I swing open the door and eye the crowd, looking for anyone I might know, anyone I might be able to squeeze some money out of in any way, but with this sorry lot, the chances are slim. The radio blares heavy, oddly in harmony with the sound of the patrons who fill the bar. I love old radios, that distinctive sound, like you are listening to music that has found itself lost in a dream. It fills me with a sort of reconnection to the world, a connection I feel is lost along with the loss of radio, a communal experience discarded ironically along with the advent of that globalizing force.

The moment I walk in, Travis from 8th street tries to grab my attention.

"Aye, yo Rick! You make those bitches bite the headboards last night?"

I chuckle.

"You know I don't fuck bitches with headboards."

"My nigga!" He lets out a hearty laugh.

25

I shake his hand on my way to a table in the corner.

The fat cackles off the grill and the aroma gets my juices flowing. There is nothing quite like indulging in a little gluttony after a multi-day drug binge. The guttural instincts of the stomach kick right past the false chemical make-up you've caked over the brain the moment seared pig flesh hits the back of your nostrils. Carnality is awakened; it's quite a sight to behold. The junkie has no time for chewing, plasm seeps out of every sagging pore, softening the food as the esophagus glops down the pulpy mash with no consideration for the tongue or mouth.

I take a seat at a booth next to the window so I can observe the freaks, birthed by this planet, walk up and down the street, doing everything and going nowhere. I love the freaks of this world, at least they keep things interesting. Can't say much for the rest of them. Everyday I see all these people working aimlessly towards trying to live longer, and yet they can't seem to figure out what they want to do on a boring Sunday afternoon. Humanity, it seems, is filled with people looking for someone to tell them what to do, and the people willing to do it. I am surrounded by men and women who have reached the age of twenty and have already had enough of life. It makes me sad. It makes sense.

An old tweaker loudly interrupts my flow of thoughts with a musing to his friend about cars.

"I wish I knew more about cars than I did. I like driving them and I like the way they look; that's about it."

He says this with an ironic bravado, oddly proud of the homeliness of his ignorance.

"Baby I Need Your Loving" by The Four Tops comes on over the radio. It strikes me in a special place as only a good Motown song can. I want to comment about it to the waitress, but I stop myself when I realize I might be becoming that old man in the bar. "They just don't write them like this anymore," I would say. The perky young waitress would scoff it off as I have scoffed many times upon hearing such things in my youth. The cycle would hopefully continue, but I decide not to say anything at all.

The place is packed, and only a single waitress scuttles around in a frenzy dealing with the demands of the people. Despite her body being filled with energy, her hollow eyes seem to scream in agony. Life has chewed this woman up and spit her back out, carving deep wrinkles into her sullen face as a sort of sick signature. She looks to have an entire lifetimes worth of persecution etched onto her face, or perhaps she is just having a bad day. One can never tell.

I open up a book of Philip K Dick short stories to kill some time while I wait for her to make her way to my table. I don't get more than two sentences in when my attention is drawn to the door as the bell attached to the top clangs. In walks Mia, wearing the same worn out clothes she had on the night before, hair almost dripping with grease.

God damn, I love a woman who doesn't give a shit. She climbs up on a bar stool at the service counter, and I send a quick prayer of thanks to the fates before grabbing the stool to her left.

"You know, you really know how to make a guy feel special," I taunt.

"Huh?"

"It's Rick. We met last night at Johnny's. It's Mia, right? Honestly, I'd be surprised if you remember me at all. You were pretty zonked."

She turns her head back to the menu in front of her with a slight look of annoyance.

I throw my book onto the counter between us in frustration.

Despite clearly trying to hide it, she looks over the book with curiosity.

"That man is a god damn virtuoso of psychedelic paranoia," she says seemingly to no one.

"Dick?" It takes a second to collect myself and realize things might not be over for me quite yet.

"Yeah, have you seen the trailer for *A Scanner Darkly*? It looks like it might be good, but I'm hesitant to get excited since every other film adaptation of his has failed to capture his genius."

Thrown by this brutal clash in opinions, it takes me a second to formulate a response, although honestly, I'm just glad she started talking. I could listen to her talk shit on my mother all night if it was in that beautiful voice.

"Oh come on, how can you not be a fan of Blade Runner?" I counter.

"Don't get me wrong, Blade Runner's a fantastic film, probably the closest anyone's gotten to portraying the atmosphere of his books. But let's be honest, it didn't even scratch the surface of the genius in that book. I mean how could they leave out the mood organ!? It's easily the most compelling part of that book. The idea that someone could schedule periods of depression and then the fact that if they don't schedule a reset time they might never want to stop wallowing in that depression is a fascinating psychological concept to me. No one has captured the allure of depression like that. No one seems to understand that once depression has eliminated all emotion, the cure could be in arms reach and you wouldn't even see the point in putting in the effort to enact it; no one but PKD, and I think it's a travesty Ridley Scott left that out of the film."

"You're not wrong, but I really think that's more a restriction of the medium itself. Plus, let's get real, Scott didn't know what the hell he was doing with that film. There are, what, five versions?" I guess, praying I'm correct.

"Six... Some people say seven if you count the work print."

"Jesus. Wait, how did I end up arguing your point?"

"I dunno, I guess I'm just good like that," she says with a smirk. It's the first time I've seen her smile since we met, and I can't take my eyes off of it.

"I just feel like art..." She pauses to think. "Not just art, but life... Life pleads to all of us for extremity, and it just seems to me that when you get to the point where ecstasy marches on with the rest of the mundane, sometimes all you can do is succumb to the abyss."

She quickly looks down in embarrassment.

"Sorry, sometimes I forget to consider my audience. Can you relate to that at all?"

"No need to ever apologize to me for speaking your mind. I don't think you would believe how much I relate if I told you. Yet, there does seem to be a side of me I don't think I could ever see getting tired of pleasure. If anything I just embrace the absurdity of it all. I'm just along for the ride." I chuckle lightly and a brisk smile crosses her face. I can tell I am the first person in a while she has conversed with who didn't recoil at her morose perception of life.

It's nice, and sadly suspicious, when things just click. It's hard to believe life is throwing you one for free, but I guess sometimes it does that.

"Hey, you wanna ditch this place and go for a walk? I think I've got a joint in my car. We can get high and see where the day takes us." I say, breaking the silence. The proposition leaves me dangling vulnerable, especially without the confidence afforded to me by the opiates. The silence before her response feels like an eternity.

"Yeah, that'd be nice."

Her response jets me forward with a joy unlike any other.

She slides off the bar stool with excitement and walks toward the door. As she passes, I can feel her sexual essence radiate through my veins. The hairs on my body prick up as if pulled by a static connection.

As I walk outside, I throw on my neon white John Lennon sunglasses and unbutton my shirt. The warmth of the sun and cool gentle breeze bring the day to a beautiful place of homeostasis. The rays beam white off Mia's porcelain skin, skin so pale I can see right through it.

We stroll past the old junkers and motorcycles that plague the parking lot and over to my silver Grand Marquis. I open the passenger side door and open the glove box, digging around for the joint. Mia eyes the car down and leans her head inside.

"This might be a silly question, but you aren't a cop, are you?"

I can tell she had become accustomed to living with the world at arm's length.

"Why the fuck does everyone always ask that... Bunch of paranoid mother fuckers, the lot of you. This car has given me more trouble in the drug game then you could imagine. I'm not even sure getting it for free was worth it anymore. Anyways, I'd have to be a pretty bad cop to have these."

I grab a half-empty bag of rigs from my glove box and chuck them out towards Mia. She catches them and examines the bag, her face a blend of fear and intrigue.

"What's it like?"

"What's what like?"

"Shooting up."

"You've never done it?"

"No." As she says this, the inflection in her voice changes entirely. A startling innocence comes over it which causes me to hesitate with a response. I pause a moment and ruminate over how to progress.

"You'll never go back... Let's just leave it at that."

"Does it hurt?"

"A bit, but you come to enjoy the sting. It grows to signify what's to come."

"Come on, tell me... I can handle it." What little resolve I have left melts away the moment I look back and see those big hazel eyes begging me. In this moment, I realize that this coupling would change both of us forever, and probably not for the better.

"You absolutely sure you want to know?"

She nods.

I bring her arm into the sun to see her veins more clearly, slowly tightening my grip around her bicep, which spikes her blood pressure. My finger caresses her rising vein, moving upwards toward the crook of her arm. For a needle junkie, veins take on a sort of fetishistic nature. I start to get hard.

"This is where we would go in. As I said, you would feel a slight sting, but that passes quickly. First the heroin kicks you right in the back of the throat. There is nothing more delicious in this world."

I wrap my fingers around the back of her neck and slowly move my thumb down her throat. She exhales slowly, releasing a breathy moan. Her face grows flush and her eyes beg me to continue.

"The taste seems to drip right down your esophagus, and with it, warmth and physical comfort matched by nothing in this world. As this is happening, every piece of mental pain, every neurosis, every care and worry in your world dissipates from your brain as if they never existed and will never exist again. The world is paradise, and those of us lucky enough to experience gods's love live there -forever- ignorant of good and evil. But always at a price."

I bring my hand up the back of her neck until I am cradling the side of her face. Her eyelids hang heavy as if she can feel what i'm describing. I lean in and our lips unite in a soft dance; she licks my bottom lip and bites it as we release. She rises slightly, cradling her nose next to mine. The warmth of her breath against my top lip makes my head heavy in the moment.

She whispers "And what's the price?"

Her voice is soft and raspy and drips with sex. Any remnants of a conscience is muted as she slides her hand up my thigh and kisses me again.

Needle virgins are my weakness. All men have them, and this is mine. There is a power there, knowing that you are forever linked with the introduction to a bliss unmatched, that I am the mediator between this great power and another soul. It's a penetration stronger than deflowering and I can see in her eyes that it is now inevitable for her. In some twisted way, I know she would be better off doing it with me - or at least, that's the justification I sell myself.

4 | Carnal Hysteria

The past fades as my awareness of the present situation returns heavy.

I grab the syringe off the table and inspect it closely. There seems to be two liquids inside, one not wanting to touch the other, a pale yellow fluid is forced above a more viscous brown one.

"Alright, look babe..." I say. "We have no idea what this is or what kind of fucked up mixture of drugs are inside it. The last thing I'm going to do is relapse on some mystery cocktail."

Mia gives me a puzzled look.

"So what's the plan?"

"I'm going to hit up Mason; he usually has all kinds of purity test kits. We'll see if anything comes up. In the meantime, you need to get clean."

Mia shoots from confusion to anger. This is not surprising as it is at the very core of an addict's will to continue use and to stave off junk sickness at all costs.

"What the fuck do you mean get clean? I thought you were in this with me."

"I never said I wasn't, but fuck going back to the way things were. If we are in this together, then you can't be trying to postpone junk sickness twenty-four seven while I'm chipping. Look, I'll make it as painless as possible: we can do it here. I'll taper you down with Sub, and I've got plenty of Xanax and other goodies for when you hop off that. You will barely feel a thing. Once we are on the same level, we can continue as planned. You don't have to stop forever; I just don't want you dependent on the shit is all..."

"You know you did this to me, right? Get the fuck off your high horse." She falls silent and exudes a state of angry contemplation.

The stages of grief have nothing on the fucked up roller coaster that is facing junk sickness. Mia just shot through the shock, denial, and anger in a matter of minutes, and I'm ashamed to admit how many blow jobs I've accepted from her for junk. So I can tell you, bargaining won't be far behind. When I turn her down for that, she will most likely swing back into anger, and when that fails I won't just get depression, but pity. Nothing quite stings more than sitting with the one you love while she bawls her eyes out.

She grabs my leg firmly, and even though it takes a second, I move her hand away.

"Come on, babe, you know chipping is better than the shit you're doing now."

Most people believe chipping is a junkie myth, a delusion the junkie falls prey to in order to keep denying the severity of their problem. After the shit portrayal book and movies have given heroin, and hell, even in society - no one believes that heroin can be done without the user falling into addiction, sickness, and despair. In reality, only ten percent of those who use opiates ever become addicted. Chipping's ultimate goal is to prevent physical dependency, and it can be done if a person follows these rules precisely. I call it the 8/72 system. A heroin user can get high for eight hours uninterrupted every seventy two hours without falling into physical addiction. For it to work, you must wait a solid seventy-two hours between each eight-hour session, cut and dry. No breaking up your eight hours into four-hour sessions within the seventy-two hours, and absolutely no combining eight-hour sessions at the end of one seventy-two hour period and the beginning of another. The problem is most drug users hold a natural abhorrence for rules or are too ignorant to understand the neurological science behind it all. This ironically leads them to try to "outsmart" the system, which in turn leads to the junk outsmarting them.

I have pushed all in with my offer to Mia and she hasn't said a word. If I had told her she had to stay completely clean for good, I doubt there would be even a moment of contemplation. She would probably walk out the door and choose the heroin. I know this because I have been given the same choice. Heroin always wins, but nostalgic thinking is a powerful force, and planting the idea that we can go back to the way things were - not just in our relationship, but in our lifestyle as well - could be enough to tip the scales.

She continues to sit in silence, not displaying a single ounce of happiness about the choice I am forcing her to make. This is new for her, which might be a good thing.

"Come on babe, we can't let the drugs rule our minds," I say with a hint of forced compassion.

I hope she doesn't see that I chuckle to myself when the words leave my mouth. The truth of it is that the drugs have always ruled our minds, whether it is focusing on staying on them or focusing on staying off. Most people end up jumping from one delusion to another, trading the drugs for a religion or "spirituality," forced into a happier, brighter, softer belief system that better suits a sober mind, however false it is. It seems we are always slaves to something.

The anger in her face slips away, and with it her entire facade. It happens so quickly it is hard to decipher how genuine it is. All that remains is a look of innocence I hadn't seen in eight years.

"Don't let me down babe, okay?"

"Okay."

I slide my hand behind her ear, combing each finger through her greasy, tangled hair, and pull her in for a kiss. I am happy with her decision, but it is hard for me to enjoy the moment while being conscious of how difficult the coming week will be.

She quickly jumps up onto my lap and straddles me, sparking a passion I haven't felt in years. My mind is instantly clouded, with only a single beam of light shining through. My will has devolved into a single drive: I want to be inside her, and nothing else matters in this moment. She tears off my shirt and throws it across the room. Her nails scratch down my chest, blood trailing close behind. She thrusts forward and bites the lobe of my ear, flicking it with her tongue as she releases. The sweet smell of sweat fills the air, so palpable I can almost feel the beads landing on my tongue. She flicks open the button on my jeans and I tear her shirt upwards and over her head. I dive into her chest, tonguing around her nipple, as she licks her palm and shoves her hand down the crotch of my pants. What little breath I have left leaves my lungs and my chest rapidly expands to catch up with the rapid firing of explosions in my brain.

This all happens so quickly, it feels as if neither of us are in control any longer. I slowly reach down the front of her pants, and inches away, she stops my arm. I look deep into her eyes, and they tell me everything I need to know. I rip my arm away from her grasp and my fingers slide in. She tightens her thighs around me and her back arches, her lips releasing a sigh of ecstasy. I lean her all the way back onto the coffee table and peel off her pants. She drips onto the table and I hover over her for a moment.

I take hold of her throat, each finger taught, cutting off the flow of blood in her neck and as I penetrate her, all divisions are melted. I tear through her, devouring every bit of flesh with a hunger that cannot be satiated. We push and pull each other, our muscles creating a brash ebb and flow. The nerves in my chest scream as she nails through my skin again, this time deeper and more intensely. She begs me to hit her and, without hesitation, I bring my palm across her face, my fingers leaving a bright rosy imprint. My sadism forms a parasitic relationship with my masochism as the pain from her scratches fuels my desire to return the favor. The pain and pleasure centers in my brain light up like a pinball machine, jolting me forward. Carnal hysteria is awakened, each of us animals, feeding off the pain and pleasure we can cause each other, barking at the moon.

She rolls me off the table. My back cracks as I hit the floor and the back of my head feels warm and wet. I reach back to check the wound; crimson fingers fill my view as my sight grows hazy and dim. This does not seem to impede Mia in the least as she quickly repositions, sliding my cock back in, which in turn snaps me right back to consciousness. She rides me vigorously, and I can tell she is about to reach her peak. Every muscle in her body tenses up and she anchors her arm around my throat. My consciousness starts to slip away again, the wound on my head throbbing to the beat of my heart as oxygen fails to make its way to my brain, but my mind is too pre-occupied to utter a word. Systems shut down and my body lays lifeless, but Mia gets so wrapped up in her climbing rapture that she doesn't even take a hint of notice. She continues to grind herself out, moaning and wailing on my comatose flesh. Her body twitches violently and then collapses limp. She lays her head on my chest, panting, slowly trying to make her way back to reality.

I awake to a prick in my arm.

"God Dammit..." I say defeated.

Mia is saddled over me bare-chested, sticking me with a needle full of what I can only hope is heroin. Before my anger can complete its genesis, she pushes in the plunger. I drift slowly down into the white cotton sheets of my bed, and I am mesmerized by the beauty inherent in the way the sunlight dances off the specks of dust in the air. How can discarded human flesh be so beautiful?

"Now don't be a little baby, just take the loss and enjoy the heroin," she says with a smirk.

"You are one crazy bitch, you know that?"

"Don't act like, deep down, you don't love it."

It's hard to argue with that.

She leans into me and lovingly caresses my chest with her cheek, and all is perfect in the world.

This doesn't last a minute before she rolls over. This saddens me - it seemed it wasn't years earlier we could just lay together, content for hours. Luckily, the sadness flows away with the heroin tide. She begins to cook up another shot on the nightstand beside her, quickly and with the precision of someone who has done it a thousand times before, making sure to suck every last drop out of the cotton before she places the rig in my hand.

"Do me, like the old days," she says with pleading look in her eyes.

I tried to flex my muscle earlier, but it is clear who is in control here. I unhook the belt from my arm and fasten it to hers. Her veins pop up bright blue against her pale skin. I slap them a few times for good measure. A beautiful plume of crimson blood dances through the burnt umber elixir, a beautiful ballet of weightlessness. I let it linger for a second before I push in and release the belt. She collapses back into my arms and we cradle each other happily in the pool of blood my wound has created in the pillow.

Here I lay, desiring normalcy but stuck on the fringes, fated to a life of delusion, and as much as I like to think I am in control, and continuously try to exercise that control, everyone in the end is driven by human banalities. The thoughts drift through my mind, unable to stick, as I behold the grace of her face, devoid of any stress or suffering.

She returns from the clouds and kisses me gently.

"You know that was a pretty fucked up thing for you to do?" I say sharply.

She chuckles at my feigned anger.

"Yeah, but aren't you glad I did?"

I search, but I can't find any discord in my heroin soaked brain, all that exists is utter joy and contentment. I flash a devious smile. I knew I was back, I knew we were back. The Dragon and the Whore.

Through the shadows I can't find her eyes, but I kiss her and start to speculate on what comes next.

"Alright, let's do another shot and head over to Mason's," I say. "I dunno about you, but I wanna find out what the fuck is up with that bone syringe."

She snatches my face with both hands and kisses me in an act of victory.

I've found that when a person is hooked on junk, they are no longer themselves; they are the very personification of junk itself. It wasn't Mia celebrating; it was the junk that drove her, exulting in its ability to pull me back into its tasty, masturbatory frenzy.

5 I.

An ill- righteous scene, cunt rags skuzz along the grooves, I can't hack it.

6 | The Gameshow

We hit the streets and head down Vista Park Drive past The Green Gill. Mason's place isn't but a couple blocks down. I walk whenever I can, as I find that avoiding any sort of driving in this city is always a good idea if it's an option.

Grey clouds loom low and heavy in the sky above and diffuse what little light this city has to give, flattening the streets and buildings into a two-dimensional dreamscape. Even the vibe of activity around us feels monotone. Citizens meandered along seemingly drained by the lack of sunlight. Skidding trash, carried by the wind barreling between the skyscrapers, is the only life this city seems to offer at the moment. Old condoms trickle down past our feet in the sewer line below, leaking milky jissom, flowing over used lottery tickets and bent needles. This city is a cesspool, but it's my cesspool and god damn if I don't love it.

Mia and I nodded out for a little too long before we left, and trying to leave her arms was as difficult as leaving a warm bed on a cold day. The junk is already starting to wear off and my nihilism is creeping back to the surface. I look Mia in the eyes and smile, but in this moment it sparks nothing inside. I'm well aware that crawling back to her this time has done nothing but enslave me in more ways than one. It's a strange paradox, even though I know in my heart that my love for her still lives, I feel absolutely nothing.

Every human being I pass I despise more than the last, part of me envious of their deluded lifestyle and part of me wishing they would all just wake the fuck up. I ponder on the illusory nature of the mind, holding so many people captive in a state of delusion that it disgusts me. If the world could just accept who they really are and not hold themselves to this divine standard, then the problem of hypocrisy might finally dissolve. The advent of imagination in human beings has been a double-edged sword; without it, we wouldn't have the lyricism of wit, the only thing that seems to give life any meaning, but at the same time it has trapped humanity in the snare of false ideals and utopias. Hypocrisy at its core is a detachment from reality, as is every religious or spiritual belief; humanity has created an unreachable dream and flagellated itself upon continued failure to reach it. Maybe mankind is fated to play out this masquerade, because it is too painful not to, but I refused to be a part of it, and I refused to pacify my derision.

46

The whole world is an absurd hoax, run on false authority. Society has set up a false power system, and upon being born into it, without choice, they expect you to follow every rule. The only right man truly holds is the right to die. Yet they expect you to swallow every masked manipulation with a smile.

Emptiness defines everything. We fill our lives with activities; activities in which we create an inflated level of importance to satiate our desire for meaning. It's hard to tell when I get like this if my eyes are opened or closed, not knowing if I'm blinded by a wall of delusion or have tapped into a secret vein of the universe.

This line of thinking unleashes a torrent of suicidal thoughts into my mind. I consider just ending the absurdity of it all, riding hard to the near end. What would I do, how would I go out? Would I kill one of these strangers, ending his miserable existence, watching the life melt out of his eyes? Murder has always been a curiosity of mine. But then what? They would brand me a psychopath, and yet I feel like the only sane person here. I'd be left in the same dilemma I started in, wondering what the point of an impact is when it's all going to be erased eventually. Like a domesticated cat who finally catches that mouse, fueled by the specter of a biology it doesn't adhere to anymore, completely unsure of what to do now that the task is done.

I chuckle to myself as I realized what a joke life is, even in death. How, when acting upon the freedoms of action suicide would grant me, I wouldn't even get to stick around to see the fallout.

I am a prisoner to life's absurdity. I can't find a reason to live, nor can I find one to die. I guess true nihilism is feeling the emptiness in your soul and gracefully embracing it as natural. No, fuck that, I didn't sign a contract. There is no grace in existence. There was no consent given to allow myself to be thrust out of a peaceful state of non-existence into this meat grinder. I am no more than a slave to life, bound against my will to live and cooperate with my captors. I take solace in the fact that no matter how bad things look now, we all get to die eventually.

"Are you fucking listening?" Mia had been talking this entire time and I had not heard a word she had said.

"Huh? Yeah babe, I just got distracted. Repeat that last bit."

She exhales a sigh that screams bitter disappointment.

"Forget it, we're here."

As we approach the stoop, I see Clint sitting, as always, like a permanent fixture outside Mason's door. He seems to be there every time I show up; I sometimes wonder if he ever leaves. Clint is probably in his late 50's if I had to guess. He wears a long brown beard with grey streaks consuming the dark pigment with every day that passes. Clint has been doing junk since Nam'. He came back and was one of the few who never stopped. The clothes on his back are saturated with sweat, fermenting since the day he had put them on and never took them back off. The white t-shirt under his green military jacket clings to his chest as if it has bonded on a biological level; hairs seem to grow out of the fabric organically. You could smell his stench from blocks away; it kicks like rock salt. I've heard stories of blind junkies across the city following the rancid scent like a homing beacon, sniffing like bloodhounds to secure their daily fix. But despite appearances, Clint continues to exude the essence of a monk: completely content to sit below the same stoop day in and day out, nothing but peace bleeding out of his mouth.

I throw two cigarettes his way as we walk past into the stairwell and share a light nod, junkie to junkie.

I knock on Mason's door, rapping in a soft staccato rhythm so he is aware that we are friendlies. He waits long enough to answer that I consider just turning around and leaving, but just as I start to turn away, he pulls the door open. He always was a paranoid motherfucker, although I guess if anyone has reason to be, it's Mason.

"Fuck dude, what year is it? This Gameshow has got to be fucking with my head; Rick and Mia together again, never thought I'd see the day. Well... Fuck, get on in here."

Mason looks like he has taken the psychonaut ship a planet too far. You know the type, constantly sporting a bath robe or a baja hoodie, always a step behind in thought, but in a way that makes him pretty endearing. It looks as if the drugs had taken their toll since we had last been together. His skin sags off his bones as if he was misfitted by the good lord himself and dark rings hang heavy below his eye sockets, pulling them so low I could see the void behind his eyes.

It's hard to tell if his apartment is housed by someone who had lost their mind or just has trouble organizing it. Papers are scattered across the room, indiscriminate of surface, and white chalk covers every inch of the wall in chemical structures and formulas. He wasn't a good friend but he was my friend. I'd say all a man can ask for is a few friends who at the least pretend to want to help and who like to indulge in the same sins.

"I just sparked up a blunt, you guys want a hit?"

"Nah, we're good" I say.

"How 'bout some MXE? Wanna play the gameshow?"

MXE is a dissociative in the vein of ketamine or PCP; we called it the gameshow because of its low threshold. You can do a key bump and you never know what you're going to get. One bump could get you comfortably buzzed, then the next time you find yourself stuck in the introspective nightmare of a psychedelic hole. It's tempting, I do love playing, but we have business to attend to.

"Nah man, we're straight." I say, trying not to offend him.

I signal to Mia to go use the bathroom so I can try to talk to Mason in private. She gets the hint.

Mason doesn't try to hide the fact that he's checking Mia out as she walks away.

"Dude, it must be unreal fucking that girl, like seeing through space and time and shit."

"Yeah, it's something else." I attempt to mask the disgust in my voice. "Don't tell Mia" I take a quick hit off the blunt.

"Ahh, it's like that with her, is it? Fucking women, man. Don't worry, man, you've been my friend a lot longer than I've known her. So what brings you around?"

"You got any of those purity tests lying around? I'd like to buy a couple off ya."

Mia returns from the bathroom and sits close beside me.

"Yeah, I've got some around here somewhere. You know the drill, fifteen bones per test. Whatcha got?"

Mia starts to pull the bone syringe out of her purse, but I signal her to stop. Maybe I'm paranoid, but even with a trusted friend I don't feel right revealing what she had stolen.

"It's just some H, wanna make sure it's not cut with fent or anything." I say.

Fentanyl is a very potent opiate often times used as cut in heroin to increase profits. I'm hoping he will buy the lie since it had been

51

responsible for hundreds of overdoses across the city in the past few months.

"Well let's see it then, I'll test it for free, and if it's straight we can do a shot," he says.

"We are in a bit of a hurry, can't I just buy one off you?" I say, pushing the lie as far as I can without seeming conspicuous.

"You come into my home after how many years, you won't do any of my drugs, and now you won't even share what you've got with me and are trying to bail on a dime. That's fucking sketch mate."

Mia leans over and whispers in my ear, "Let's just show him. I wanna know what the fuck this is."

She digs the bone syringe from her purse and unwraps it.

"Huh, well that is interesting..."

Mason's distinct lack of shock for what looks to be a syringe from another planet would be suspicious if he was sober, but it is unsettlingly suspicious for a man out of his mind on the gameshow.

"Well let me grab a test from the back and we can get started, give me a minute, I never know where I leave this shit."

Mason shoots into his bedroom and I pick up the blunt from the ashtray, take a drag, and then pass it to Mia.

"Something's wrong here, Mia," I say. "I can feel it. Mason is no stoic, and that was an unsettling attempt at keeping his cool in a situation where any normal person would have been losing their mind."

"I dunno, babe, Mason's always been hard to read. Who knows what kind of cocktail of drugs he's on at the moment?"

"Wait here, I've gotta take a piss."

"Don't do anything fucking stupid."

I softly tip-toe between trash and papers on the floor, not wanting to crush anything. I hear scuffling in Mason's room and then out of nowhere he kicks on Doolittle by The Pixies. I creep closer to the door to see if I can hear anything over the music.

"Get...*mrmmfmsmfmrm...* on the line quick"

"The master key...*mfmmfmrmrm...*yeah it's here now... *mrmrmfmsmfm...*just two junkies I know..."

"*mfrmfmmrmrm...*do you think that's necessary?"

"But...*mrmmfmrmfs...*alright, yeah don't worry about it. I'll take care of it."

I rush back to the couch as quickly and quietly as possible, which was harder than it sounds with all the shit on the floor.

"We gotta get out of here, babe. Mason was on the phone. I think he knows more than we think. I think he's in on this somehow."

"Chill babe, don't get all paranoid on me, it's a bit of a turn off. If he knows more than we do, then he can fill us in. Take another hit of the blunt and let's just wait and see."

I grab her wrist, knocking the blunt out of her hand.

"No, listen to me, I think this shit is serious, I think he was talking to whoever wants this back, I don't think we're safe."

"Listen to yourself; you seriously think Mason would hurt...?"

Before Mia can finish her sentence Mason walks into a view with a revolver in his belt. I shoot Mia a glare that says more then I told you so. Her jaw drops down and she doesn't utter a peep. Mason falls to his knees and looks to start convulsing. His head rips upwards and he starts shouting nonsense about death, about his death. There was nothing about this that lead me to believe this was a man to be feared, more so a man to be pitied, broken and suffering. He had this perverse staccato to the flow or I guess you could say lack of flow, of his language, with a variety of volumes and tones that instantly filled me with unease. His expressions could only represent a man in extreme agony, and for that very reason, I jump down to help him. I am fueled mostly by a desire to help this man any way I could, but I couldn't help but feel invigorated by the experience. I use one arm to lock him down and with the other I cup his face. I tell him to look me in the eyes, and his eyes go from being lost in blindness, to an instant connection with mine. I tell him anything he needs to hear to bring him back to any sort of contentment, comfort, or ease of being. I lie. A lot.

I know exactly where he was at in that moment, I had been a denizen of that soul wrenching place many times in my life. And by fate or chance, this was a man who had helped me escape that place many times before. He was the one to save me, and here I was trying to do the same for him, in some kind of beautiful direct Karma.

But a man can only do so much with a broken mind. He overwhelms me and draws the gun on us.

"What the fuck man, just chill the fuck out and put the gun down. We can talk this out. Just remember who you are talking too, we go back to the beginning you and I."

"Look you know I love you guys, but I'm in deeper than you can know with this shit, self-preservation and all. You understand."

"Look, if you are in trouble, maybe we can help. You got wrapped up with the wrong people, I get it. Mason, my man, just tell us what's going on. Look man, we were just trying to have a little fun, you can take the syringe. No one has to get hurt here."

"Wrong people? Wrong people? You don't understand, The Meiser Group are THE people, there is no right or wrong."

Mason looks like he was in the process of cracking psychologically; sweat collects in beads on his forehead and his hands are trembling. Clouds pass and a few beams of light shine into the room. His arms hang unnatural, as if attached to strings. I see now that this is a man clearly controlled against his will.

Mia grips my thigh, obviously unhappy about my rational instinct to talk things out rather than to fight, and my apparent willingness to give up the syringe. The force presented by Mason has raised its value in her eyes. She slowly inches her hand into her purse and pulls out a pack of cigarettes. Mason locks onto her immediately.

"Get the fuck out of your purse while I figure this out! Fuck... Fuck!" He screams with escalating volume.

"Chill, look if you are going to kill us, I need a cigarette. Oblige me that at least."

Mia hangs a cigarette from her lips and throws one my way. Always the cool one.

"Hey Mason, do you have a lighter?" Mia displays a smirk as she asks, a look of playful confidence that fills me with unease.

"Don't fucking play games with me!"

"Babe, do you have one?"

As I pat down my pockets, she pauses me.

"I think I've got one in my purse actually."

She slowly reaches into her purse and without hesitation she pulls a
gun on Mason.

Shit.

Two shots fire and my ears ring with a piercing intensity. I am
instantaneously disoriented; my mind fills with an intense confusion.
What has she done? She is a descendent of the Simian line, picking at
emotions, unaware of where they drift in from or what they could
mean. Thriving on altercation and driven by lust. Lust for an object
unidentified. My ears discern nothing but I feel a vibration shutter
through the floor. The lone sound of The Pixies slowly overtakes the
ringing in my ears and brings me back to the present.

7 | Balsamic Heroin

Silence is often equated to peace, but personally, I believe this to be a false equation. The silence I sit in thrashes the room, shaking disgust from the walls, pulling me to action. My mind is unoccupied by will, I feel myself being dragged by the collar through the trash and papers on the floor, but no one is present.

I squint in pain as Mia's blood runs warm down my face, forcing its way past crusted eye jissom and into the open windows of my soul. Bits of bone and flesh cling to my gums, wanting to flow down my puckered throat. I expel the blood in my mouth onto the wall outside Mason's room, fearing the possible cocktail of diseases that might be dripping down my throat. I felt there was no need to check either body, they were both clear shots. Mia had caught Mason in the throat and he was dead before I was able to recover from the shock. Mason, on the other hand, had caught Mia right between the lips, and if I was the Divine one above, I'd sentence him to an eternity in hellfire for destroying such a perfect piece of my art. Half of her jaw is on the floor, which left a gaping throat and eyes dangling backwards over the top of the couch, attached only by a small strand of flesh and hair. I scrape a large chunk of her lip out of the crevice of my clavicle. One last kiss. I make a quick smirk as the dark joke pops through my head and then immediately find myself pulled back into the situation at hand.

I crawl my way into Mason's room and climb rung by rung up his shelving, weighed heavy by the souls whose body lay untethered in the other room. I use all the strength in my body to reach up to the top shelf and grab Mason's stash box, and once I have it in my grasp, I let go. The fall feels slow but the crash is fast and heavy. Mason's drugs and works scatter across the floor. I eye a few bags of heroin, stamped with black M's, and a new rig. After I drag myself and the works over to Mason's metal bed frame, I prop myself up against it.

The spoon shakes violently in my hand as I hold my arm steady to keep the heroin from spilling over. I search my pockets for a lighter, and having no luck, decide this isn't the moment to care. So I cold cook the mixture, stirring it slowly with the plunger of my rig.

My blood is pumping so fast that I have no need to tie off. I dig the needle deep into my vein. The blood forces the plunger up and I force it back down along with the solution. My pupils pin and all anxieties from the event are expelled from my body. I look over at the chunks of cartilage, flesh, and bone hanging off my shoulder with complete detachment and flick them onto the floor one by one.

I meander into the bathroom and start the shower. Footprints of blood follow close behind across the white tile floor. I peel my blood soaked shirt off my back and toss it into the corner along with the rest of my clothing. It lands with a squish.

As the hot water rushes over my scalp, a weight seems to lift off my shoulders. It feels incongruent with the current situation, but I can't help but feel free. I have always relished being alone, completely content with full freedom of will, unimpeded by the will of others. Companionship is nice but it can be sorely overrated at times. Plus, it's nice to know that I ultimately wasn't responsible for Mia's death after all.

I start to feel sick that the heroin allows these perversions of thought and feeling to exist in my brain at all, and even sicker as they do nothing to shake the emotional ruin that still lingers behind the heroin in my mind.

The blood drips off my skin, spirals down the drain, and with it goes the past. I exit the shower clean, but in no way refreshed. While scavenging through Mason's closet for some threads to wear out I realize that my prints have to be all over this place. This thought bothers me little until I realize that out of Mason's droves of daily clients; I am really just one in a sea of junkies, and that's if any cop decides it is even worth their time to investigate the death of a few lowlife drug users. I pocket the rest of Mason's stash and fish through both his and Mia's wallets for any cash they might have on them.

A hundred and some change isn't a bad score.

I am practically out the door when I get the feeling that I might be forgetting something. A dissonance falls over the room; something wasn't right. Oddly enough, the bodies seem to fit perfectly in this hellhole, but I feel a sharp prick in the back of my mind as I glance over the bone syringe still sitting on the table, untouched by the chaos that had gone on around it.

"I'm not quite done with you yet," I say under my breath.

I wrap it back up in cloth and place it in my chest pocket.

As I exit the stairwell, I throw Clint a few bags of H to buy his silence, although I doubt he would say anything either way.

"Hey Rick, two guys came by all suspicious like. Be careful out there," Clint says in a rare moment of expression.

I throw Clint another bag.

"Thanks for the heads up friend. I'll do my best."

Paranoia strikes heavy as I ponder everything that has gone down. Who was The Meiser Group? What were they doing with this syringe? Why am I being followed?

It isn't hard to feel in present danger.

The muscles in my legs seem worthless as gravity pulls my skeleton down the city streets. Buildings perforated by broken windows pass in front of my eyes as I drift down into the east side; the smell of musty sea water wafts heavy through the air. I notice a figure in the alleyway ahead. I can't help but think that he's there for me, but I try to continue on and push the paranoia out of my head. Relief rains down as I pass him, albeit preemptively.

"There you are you little prick," the man yells as I walk by.

I turn around to see Mia's brother Byron. Byron is looking more punk than usual. I'd say he has slept in his tattered jeans and t shirt a few too many nights, but the shadows under his eyes say different --he couldn't know, could he?

"Byron! What's up buddy?" I try to act as normal as possible.

"Don't give me that 'buddy' shit. I know you are responsible for what happened to Mia last week. I can't prove it yet, but I know you were involved. You are always involved. Coincidentally you've been there for every shitty day in her life." Byron screams with an anger riddled with adrenaline.

"Last week? What are you talking about? I haven't seen Mia in months." I find myself genuinely puzzled.

"Don't play dumb with me. You know damn well Mia OD'd last week, and I'm telling you man, you better watch your back, because the moment I can prove you were the little shit who did it, you are going to be in a ditch on the lower east side."

Byron runs back into the shadows of the ally and leaves me worse off then I was before.

An indistinct voice comes from the alleyway as I walk on.

"I know you killed her!"

Was I hearing things, or was that the paranoia speaking?

There's no way Byron could know about today, and if he did, why would he be focusing on an overdose from a week ago? The details didn't add up. I keep walking, stunned from the experience, with a general sense of discord in my mind.

It isn't long before I find myself outside The Temple of Fuck and standing beside the front door is a nubile young woman, smoking a cigarette. Even though she's wearing a heavy beige overcoat, she seems to exude pure, uncut sex. She knows she is dripping with it, and revels in the fact that she causes men to languish in their inability to join her in the sexual bath. I'm happy enough just to be soaking in her carnal vibes.

I make my way inside, pull up a seat at the bar, and flag down Frank. A lone catatonic drunk lingers at the end of the bar, lazily soaking in alcohol through his fingers.

"Hey, how ya doin' Rick?"

"It's been a weird one, Frank."

"You don't say."

"Mia's dead."

"Well shit... A typical junkies exit?"

"Anything but. Don't really wanna get into it though."

"Sorry to hear that Rick, I know how much she meant to you. Drinks are on me tonight."

"Thanks Frank. Double rum on the rocks if you wouldn't mind."

"Right away."

"Fuck... I guess that's just how it goes. Either everything works out, or it doesn't. Today seems to be one of those days that it doesn't. Don't think I'll ever get use to it. Who's Pauly got working right now?"

"Jessica, Samantha, and Nicole I think."

"Nicole? Is she new?

"Just started last week."

"How is she?"

"Total knockout, brunette, right up your alley."

I palm Frank a hundred and he hands me a room key. Room 23.

"Thanks, Frank."

"No problem Rick. Don't do anything I wouldn't do."

"We both know that's a pretty short list."

I shoot Frank a smirk and he chuckles. Red beads hang over the back doorway which leads to Pauly's back rooms. The beads wash over me as I stroll through into the short hallway beyond. Iron doorknobs hang on blood red doors which line the black brick hallways, all dimly lit by iridescent lanterns.

The décor escapes my grasp. All of it is obviously thought up by flaccid pricks reinforcing the idea that they are doing something immoral by painting the place to look like Satan's playground; the more iniquitous the hotter it is to them.

Moans and shrieks reverberate off the walls and down the hallway. I wade through a cacophony of pain and pleasure, unable to distinguish one from the other.

I find room twenty three and go to enter. The metallic doorknob is cold to the touch. Before I can fully enter, my body is pulled inside and flung onto the bed by Nicole. She slams the door closed behind her.

"Thank God you made it, do you have the master key?!" She says with intensity.

It's the girl who was outside smoking; I am both overjoyed and a little confused. Stockings rose up her legs, clinging to her beautiful skin, and end leaving the perfect amount of thigh flesh to grace my vision. Garters attach the stockings to her corset which causes her perfect breasts to pop out like an old 3D movie trick. Although the outfit is stunning, I can't help but feel it doesn't suit her.

"Honey, you gotta be careful. I'm a lot older than I look," I say.

"Did you bring the key?"

"Whoa, baby, we just met. I usually like a little small talk before we get into the role-play."

"Rick, you don't have to worry about that, they aren't listening. This is a clean room."

"Baby, you and I both know nothing Pauly touches is clean," Just as the words escape, I realize she shouldn't know my name.

"Rick, The Intransigence has a new assignment for you."

What the fuck is she talking about? I let her continue.

"You've completed the first part of your assignment. You've secured the master key; do you have it with you?"

I have an immediate recall to what I heard Mason talking about over the phone.

"Yeah, it's safe." I hope she won't catch on to the fact that I have no clue what she is going on about.

"Good. Look, Rick, The Meiser Group has taken hold of a large part of the Provax Zone. The Intransigence has sent word that you need to use your cover along with the master key to gain access to the Provax Zone and report back with your findings. Everything you will need to know is in this report."

I place the manila envelope on the bed to my left, still trying to grasp everything.

"The Provax Zone?"

"Rick, I know you've gotten deep in with The Meiser Group, befriending Mason Sellers from as early as ten years ago. God, I can't imagine what it's been like, but you can't forget who you really work for, what *we* are working for. You are an invaluable asset to The Intransigence. If you are going to aid us in finding the cure for The Sickness, then you have to listen to me."

I start fingering through the rolodex of my memories, most of which are obscured by heavy drug use or have just faded with time. I start to question my own mind. Did Mason mix some type of hallucinogen in with those bags of heroin? Could she be telling the truth? Have I really lost myself to an undercover identity? Have I been

67

searching for the cure all along? Deep in my subconscious, I feel she was telling the truth, and for some unknown reason, I decide to roll with that.

I focus on her as she moves closer to the bed. She sits down tight to my side and comfort eases down my spine as she slowly rubs her hand up my thigh. It is hard to fight against the path of least resistance. She moves in inches from my face, and looks me dead in the eyes; I can feel her breath meet mine.

"Rick, if you don't want to do this for The Intransigence, then do it for me, for everything we've put into this." She picks up the bone syringe and places it in my hands. "People are coming for you Rick. You need to take this and leave for Central City. Use it to get into The Land of Nod. You will know what to do once you are there, you always do."

I look at her with confusion.

"You are telling me all this is just to get into some nightclub?"

"Rick, The Provax Zone is all around us, but the only way to enter it, to be aware of it, is to inject this syringe into the bloodstream. Only then can your neurological pathways be opened to what's already there. It is imperative you inject yourself and meet up with the head of the The Intransigence. We have already set up this meeting and he is expecting you. We won't get this opportunity again. His name is Dr. Lee, and you will find him at a club called The Land of Nod in Central City. Your flight leaves tomorrow. As I said everything you need to

68

know is in this report. Look, it's important you don't inject this until you arrive in Central City. It only lasts so long."

"You want me to bring this fucking thing through airport security?"

"You and I both know you've smuggled worse then that, and it's the only surefire way we can get you into The Provax Zone and The Land of Nod. So buckle up, champ."

The Land of Nod... How poetic. Am I Cain, cursed by god to wander endlessly east of Eden? Or perhaps I've always been a resident.

"Spend the night here with me. Maybe I can help you remember why we are doing this. We can discuss the details and... Reminisce. I want to know your soul again."

"Baby, I sold my soul to the devil a long time ago and, sadly, he paid out."

I feel her hand move farther up my thigh. She leans in and kisses me with lips that make me feel at home, bringing with them an eerie sense of nostalgia that I can't place. We fall in tandem and know each other's bodies in ways unexplainable to my present mind. It's not twenty minutes before I'm spent, lying in bed with her head on my chest.

She looks up and into my eyes.

"Do you want me to make you a shot?"

I smile.

"That sounds wonderful. Kill me just a little bit more."

I watch as she fixes me a shot and administers it with extreme precision. Not a drop is lost. Pauly's girls are always on point.

I'd be happy never to leave this bed, content with my junk filled head and Nicole on my chest.

The Land of Nod, and I, a permanent resident.

Cut.

My eyes creep open dull and sore. Instinctively, I grasp for a body beside me, but my hands feel nothing but a hollow crater left in the mattress. All that is left of her is the taste of her pussy on the back of my throat. Poetic.

Dreamy musings of the night prior shake me witless. The shivers of junk sickness start to ripple across my skin and I find myself caught in a frigid and heavy darkness, unable to think or act for more than a few seconds, as all my past illusions crack and fall away. The symptoms come on quicker and quicker the longer I have been on this shit, no matter how long I've been clean in between. The physical compulsion of my disease lifts me out of bed, and my torpid body sucks and saps what little life force it can get from the inanimate objects that surround me. I am driven purely by the single thread of desire to get well.

As I pull on my suit, the cloth clings to my sweat-soaked skin. I don't take time to tuck it in or even button it up. I grab the manila envelope Nicole left, on my way out the door, and light a cigarette as I stumble out the back exit and into the blinding noonday sun. The city screams, a single vast organism, and here I rest tightly in its asshole.

As I slide down the auburn brick wall of the alley, I whistle Jimmy over to cop a couple of bags. An old friend used to tell me "a man who breaks his own rules is a man who doesn't know what he wants," and I know well and good I'm breaking my own rules, but I decide to give myself a pass given the nature of the week. Hell, he's not wrong. I've never really known what I've wanted.

That same man once told me "there is purity in purpose," and until this moment, I don't think I ever really knew what he meant. But I think that is the allure of heroin. For once in my life, I had the drive to work for something. I had purpose, even if it was the empty, faux purpose heroin supplied me. Motivation feels good, even if it is to be the Junklord.

Passersby gasp at the site of me, mouths agape. They're disgusted by the utter lack of dignity in a piece of human sewage feverishly sticking himself. Blood runs down puckered holes which color the puddles in the pavement a deep crimson.

What would these people do without me, without the ideal I represent? How can they be right if I was not the living embodiment of wrong? They walk on egos intact, unaware of the service I have

71

provided for them. I find myself in deep isolation because of the sacrifice I have made; a street prophet dishonored by the people of his time.

Now that I'm straight, I decide it's time to get home and figure out my next move. Advertisements call out to me from above, painting every inch of real estate this city has to offer. Consumers bustle past, soaking up the propaganda fed to them, always seeking the happiness promised to them from that next purchase. Everyone is part of a market, human souls divided up into sects and pandered to by corporations; corporations that get off spoon-feeding us the illusion of choice. Not even counter cultures are free from this. We all must play this game; the only way to truly rebel is from the inside.

I arrive home, and for a second, I expect Mia to greet me, relaxed on the bed, until I spot her clothes strung along the floor and couch. The grief stings, my head aches, and for a second I am flooded with anger. I prep the second bag I scored off Jimmy. The needle is my great escape.

The T.V. blares as I toss a variety of garments into my suitcase. Tears warm and wet start to trickle down my cheeks, my physical reaction in quiet discord with the peace that is in my mind. The heroin isn't enough to keep the emotions locked away in my head. They seem to come and go erratically, bursting forth as if through a clogged pipe. I fall to my knees, let go, mind body and soul washed over with the reality that the woman I loved is gone.

Pain can be as meditative as pleasure, forcing all thoughts out of my head, causing a stark devotion to the present moment. The emotions seem to lessen the more I embrace them. Soon I collect myself and continue packing.

Who knows how long this assignment will last? Better pack the essentials. I punch in the code to my safe and remove my drug kit, placing it on the bed beside my suitcase. I will have to deal with those sadists down at the TSA, I know that much. But I'm unsure of how thorough those pigs will be, it'll be a safe bet to hide the goods.

I take a prepackaged bottle of vitamin capsules and empty them out, filling the capsules with everything from ketamine and Xanax to cocaine and DMT. I reseal the bottle and screw on the top. Next, I squeeze out a bottle of Visine and fill it with liquid LSD, which is something you could never have too much of on a case like this. I don't bother procuring any heroin as it's purer and cheaper in Central City.

I take a quick shower and, once ready, flag down a cab on the street below. It's barely past two in the afternoon and my flight doesn't leave till five, but it's imperative I make a quick stop at the bar as I always prefer to fly drunk. Being caught sober on a flight is not something I'd wish upon my worst enemies.

The only people down at the bar when I arrive are Phil Jackson, a sorry little tosspot who is always drenched in his own self-pity, and my bookie Derrick Meyers. I choose the seat next to Derrick. They don't bring much to the table, but they sure are men of easy company.

I start guzzling down Long Island Teas, placing them on Derricks tab as he still owes me a couple hundred from the Steelers game the week before.

Derrick wont stop giving Phil shit about giving an obvious con artist fifty dollars.

"What was I suppose to do, let the guy miss his grandmothers funeral?" Phil shakes out.

"There is no funeral, you dumbass!" Derrick snaps.

"At least I'll have good Karma coming my way, Derrick. You gotta think about those things," Phil says.

"Phil, you know damn well that Karma is on a bus halfway to Central City," I crack.

Phil hangs his head as the rest of us in the bar erupt into mocking laughter.

Wasn't long before the last thing I remember was getting in a verbal brawl with that prick over the coin he owed me, then throwing his glass against the wall before I left.

Before I know it I am in line at the airport and there are twenty something sad sacks between me and my ticket. My misanthropy rises. I impatiently wait to check in for the flight I somehow showed up late for. Halfway through the line ahead of me is a small brunette, who I didn't notice 'til she turned back, locked eyes with me, and then quickly turned away. Her eyes gleamed mean. I figure she's a college student, probably traveling to the Central City to "find herself." Fucking Hipster Central was more like it. She is sporting a belly shirt and a cute little hippie skirt, and has an ass that causes the baggage boys to double over in ecstasy as they try to hide the quickly spreading stains in their pants.

It's always novel to me how the sight of a beautiful woman can leave one with a sort of afterglow, a gratitude that can't help but feel empty and unfulfilled. But even that longing and desire brings with it a feeling of paradoxical joy and contentment.

The line dwindles down and I'm next. The attendant has a lost and frustrated look in his eyes as a small Cambodian woman in front of me keeps shouting in her native tongue. Anxious to find that girl, I throw myself into the fold of the commotion and demand I get on my plane.

"I don't know what all this commotion is about, but my neck is on the line here son, and if I don't make this flight my boss won't have it. It just won't do." I rant hoping my drunken confidence is enough to move the boy to action. "I'll be demoted, stuck corralling the pests in middle management the rest of my days. I'm sure you understand, so just print my ticket and I'll be on my way."

He seems so confused by the situation that any authority I projected was received as legitimate, even if it's a false, drunken authority. I hand him my passport, retrieve my ticket, and make my way through security without any hassle from the swine in TSA. They were too busy enjoying their inspection of the inner recesses of a young Indian boy to worry about the likes of me. Besides, they barely ever stop a white man in a suit if he carries himself well enough. I'm not saying the privilege is fair, but it is efficient.

I barrel through a crowd of business men, waving my ticket at the stewardess. Once I board, my eyes dart around from seat to seat, looking for the girl from earlier. I spot her heading for lavatory in the back and quickly rush over to the older Asian gentleman sitting next to her empty seat, pleading for him to switch seats with me.

"You don't understand," I say. "It is of utmost importance that I have this seat. I have health issues, you see, and if I don't have a seat near the middle of the jet, the pressure is liable to cause the rapid expulsion of bodily fluids. I won't go into much more detail than that, but it's best for everybody if I sit here."

My yarn is lost on him, so I fish a fifty out of my breast pocket and shove it in his face. He takes the money, but looks away and continues to sit. I grab his arm, ready to yank him upwards, when I notice two stewardesses near the front of the plane eyeing me with concern as well as the brunette who is now exiting the stall in the back and making her way towards me. I release his arm and swiftly fix his shirt for him, patting him gently.

"So sorry, thought you were someone else. Preflight jitters, you understand."

I grit my teeth and proceed to mumble obscenities under my breath as I take my seat next to a morbidly obese woman who smells like she has pork stored away in her fat folds for a mid-flight snack. I sink into a feeling of deep resignation and decide to pop a Xanax. Eyes closed, I fantasize about shooting my last bag of heroin with the brunette in the airplane bathroom before fucking her silly. I hope that fate will cross our paths again. Sometimes all a man needs is hope, but when hope fails, there is always distraction.

The Xanax fails to carry me through to arrival. I awaken to the sun rising in the east, scattered amongst the clouds that float along with the plane at thirty-six thousand feet. Its rays dulled by the thick plastic windows on the jet. My head is in a fog as I try to regain conscious awareness of my surroundings. My bones crack and my muscles pull taught as I contort my body into various stretches. I slump into the faux leather of the airplane seat, and my emotions slump along with me. How long can I go blissfully ignoring the truth of my reality? How long would the drugs last? I wonder. I feel hopeless with them and without them; always searching for new and better ways to distract myself from the brutish reality I seem to be a part of. Even those things that once brought beauty to my eyes are now death to me.

It's happening again. The horror I tried to claw myself free from on a daily basis is setting in. My brain sends countless signals in defense of the illusion it so loves to uphold. Am I nervous about the trip? Am I depressed about the girl? All vain attempts at disguising the dragon looming in the careless macrocosm.

I tell myself that being a slave to the drugs is different than being a slave to religion, but it isn't. It's just another way of distracting myself from the uselessness of the universe. I can't choose what I believe, but I can choose to change how I perceive it. Altering my perception through drugs seems to me the only out. It is either that or crack into madness under the pressure of the truths at play here. We all endure suffering while clinging to the ideal of progress, ignoring the madness that lays bare, putting all of our effort into building something when the only sure fact is that it will all be wiped away in the end. It's all for nothing, yet we act as if it is everything.

I've found there are two steps to life.

First you have to realize everything is meaningless. Then, you have to find a reason to live despite the piercing knowledge of that fact. Only problem is that, other than heroin, I have yet to find that reason, and the heroin, honestly, just isn't sustainable.

Suicide seems like a good option; non-existence never hurt anybody. Although, I never seemed to have the biological temperament to carry out such an option, as rational as it may have seemed.

The only option is to revel in the absurdity of it all, kick and scream at the universe, not because it could make a difference, but because in the end it wouldn't.

8 | Mercy

Here I sit, lonely but, sadly, not alone, relegated to a dive bar at the south end of Central City, drinking whatever shit beer they have on tap. The cheap discount store Christmas lights that hang above the bar somehow only makes the place more tacky. Man the holidays suck. They never used to, which only makes it worse. Memories are like little viruses swimming through my mind, taunting my present state. My choices weren't just poisoning my present and future, but my past as well. Good memories are a luxury for the presently happy, it seems.

Even though the sun had fallen a few hours earlier, I decide to continue wearing my sunglasses to keep a block on the rest of the world. While I stare endlessly at my shaking hands, I recall the past week, wondering if I have an ounce of sanity left in my broken brain.

The mission papers Nicole gave me are the final strand holding my tattered brain together. Without them, I'd surely believe the entire trip to be a mistake, a delusion, the final joke my binge was to play on me before the curtain call. I can imagine the newspaper headlines now:

"He died, broken and alone, in a rented room."

Like a scratch across my glasses, everything looks wrong from wherever I place my feet. It is not an enjoyable place to be, but it brings with it the comfort of home. I hear the door clang open behind me, but I decide it's too much effort to lift my head out of my glass to see who has entered. My nostrils perk up as an enticing aroma fills the air.

"You're the drunk from the plane, almost got thrown off for harassing that old Asian man."

"Fuck off will..." I get three words out before I finally lift my head. My nerves spring awake at the site of the girl from the plane.

"Sorry" I say with a hint of cynicism. "It's been a rough week, filled with horror and dissatisfaction."

"Sounds like you need another drink."

She signals the bartender over.

"Two more of whatever he's drinking"

"What are you drinking anyways?"

"Daiquiri."

"What, did you forget your dick on the plane?"

"Hemingway Daiquiri. I'll have you know it's a very sophisticated drink."

"Oh really, a sophisticated drink in a bar like this? Whats top shelf in this place? Bacardi?"

I chuckle.

"Well it looks to be Malibu, but I don't taste coconut so they might just be re-using that bottle. Sorry for my defensiveness, I've had a... week to say the least. Name's Rick."

"Jessa."

"Pleasure to meet you, Jessa. It will be nice to have some fateful company."

I shake her hand cordially.

"Well, I didn't exactly just come in here. I live across the street. Recognized you as you walked in."

"You can discount it all you want, it's still fate. Older I get, the harder it gets to ignore."

She eyes my shaking hands and gives me a look of concern.

"You alright there, Rick? You got the DT's?"

"Would I be shaking this bad this many drinks in if I did? As I said, I've had a week."

"You know your kinda a dick right?"

"Yeah, it seems to be a running personality trait with me. I've come to accept it."

"You know, not all girls are into that."

"Oh believe me, I don't do this for anyone else. It's all natural."

"Why don't we finish these drinks and head over to my place? I don't think this dive is helping your mindset at all," Jessa says.

Jessa is wearing sunglasses with pink reflective lenses which perfectly reflect my visage twice over. I can't get a read on her eyes but I think 'what the hell?' A silver star of David hangs cradled between her breasts, appearing almost white compared to her olive skin.

"You Jewish?"

"Yeah, well, my dad is. My mom's catholic. I think my mother would have to be the Jew for it to be official. Just got back from a student trip to Israel actually. Beautiful country."

"Nice. I'm German myself, if the blonde hair and blue eyes didn't clue you in. So if history has taught me anything, this should go flawlessly."

"Well, we can burn that bridge when we get to it."

I kick back the rest of my rum and then follow her across the street. Her apartment is trendy, doubly so for someone of her age. Concert and movie posters fill the walls -you know, "good ones"- and incense burns slowly in the corner. The furniture looks like it's straight out of the Ikea catalogue, but her decorative touches give the place plenty of personality despite that. She drops onto the couch and signals me to join her. Thievery Corporation fills the air as she fiddles with the stereo remote.

"Where ya staying?" she says

"The Reed House on 19th. It's decent enough. I'm digging your place. You live alone?"

"Yeah, I like my privacy. I can be a hella introvert at times."

"I wouldn't have known. I must be something special if an introvert came out to pull me outta the bar."

Jessa removes her sunglasses, revealing glassy red eyes.

"You're not half bad," she says with a wink. "You wanna smoke?"

"Sure, why not? You guys still getting good bud down here in Central?"

"The best. Medically grown. I'll go grab some, wait here."

I wait a few minutes but something in my gut prompts me to walk into her room; call it instinct or call it impatience, I don't really know what it was, and I sure don't care now. The night takes a turn as I open her door to reveal Jessa who is now in the process of cutting out lines of brown powder onto a mirror. She reactively tries to hide the powder as she sees me enter, but I can tell by the look on her face she knows it's too late.

"Fucking right, my girl's got some H," I say with my first expression of excitement for the night.

"Yeah..." She says hesitantly and in an embarrassed tone.

"Oh, now is no time for shame. No one likes a bashful junkie. Mind if I get a line?"

Her expression shifts from guilt to joy in nanoseconds.

"Yeah, of course. I wasn't sure if you were down with the hard shit, and don't call me a junkie."

She hands me a rolled up twenty and I bend down to snort a line.

"Don't be doing this shit with pride now... Also, not... Fucking... Bad..." I say, lifting my head up, sniffing loudly.

"I know, right? New crew came in town not too long ago, dealing out of a club called The Land of Nod. Is that not the perfect club name to deal Heroin out of? We should go some time, place is weird... Like a David Lynch movie, but the dope is good as fuck."

"You know I'm down," I say, trying to stay casual about my knowledge of the joint.

"Honestly, I wasn't sure what to make of you until now."

"Well, praise the lord. I'm reborn! And by lord, obviously I mean Satan"

"Obviously," she says with a chuckle. "We can still smoke the bowl if you want."

"Let's just lie down. This shit's hitting me pretty hard."

We climb into her bed, and as the drugs take hold I begin to feel endlessly comfortable with her. I pull her body close to mine and we seem to float together. The heat of our bodies warm the bed and I feel sparks of arousal from the warmth of her body against mine. I inch my hand up her shirt, taking hold of her breast, as I cradle her body. My breathe falls slow and heavy upon her neck and, without hesitation, I roll her onto her back. She arches forward and kisses me before I can initiate. At first, it starts slow, but despite my penchant for sensuality, I find I can't hold back. I ask and her lips answer. I am well aware that she wants this as badly as I do. Jessa inhales sharply as I penetrate her, slowly pumping to ease my cock deeper. The heroin does little to slow the rising orgasm. She forcefully grabs me by the back of my neck and looks at me with crazed, begging eyes.

"Fuck the Jew out of me, you Nazi bastard!" She screams.

I quickly stop as my mind tries to make sense of what it is hearing.

Once my mind catches up, I proceed to cum harder than I ever have in my life. It is as if the entire weight of the holocaust had burst out of my cock. She quivers and cums in tandem, reveling in my seminal load.

I pull out and roll over to the side of the bed, unsure about what the fuck just happened. She jumps up to clean off in the bathroom as if this was another Monday. I will say though, that lying in bed post coitus, confused but content, watching her naked body glide towards the bathroom feels like one of the greatest moments of my life. I feel like I am in love --God, why am I such a chump?

"Good going. I think you just made the entire Jewish race a new fetish of mine with that little performance," I say.

She chuckles.

"You're welcome."

"Can you throw me a towel?"

"Sure," she says as she tosses a crumpled towel from the corner of the room.

She sits down naked and starts to roll a spliff, her ass a perfect heart. I find the combination of weed and tobacco are unmatched post-coitus, so I am very pleased with her decision. We spark it, passing it back and forth as we lay attached in each other's arms. I am unsure how I arrived in this situation, what it all means and how it had even happened so quickly. But I am never one to investigate a good situation while I am in the thick of it. The smoke on the other hand loves to over-analyze, and I'm four hits deep. I ultimately hope this is more than just this moment. I've always felt one night stands are like confessing your sins to a stranger on the street. Not that there's anything wrong with that.

"I'm sorry," The words fall inches from her mouth.

"Shit, I'm the one who should be apologizing. I lasted, what, like a few minutes tops? Let's just say this is not me at my best. You are just something else."

She looks away in guilt.

"No, I'm sorry. I haven't exactly been honest with you."

"Fuck, you don't have AIDS, do you? I didn't even use a rubber," I quip.

She chuckles and playfully shoves me away.

"No, asshole. Look, I didn't just happen to see you walk into that bar earlier."

"What do you mean?"

"I'm your contact down here, with The Intransigence. Not that I'm not attracted to you, it's really the reason I kept the whole contact thing hidden. I kinda just wanted to have some fun before we got down to business. I hope you're not mad?"

Blood rushes up to my head, stars fill my vision, I push myself away from her, needing separation until I can reappraise the situation, 'til I can cut through this haze the drugs had formed in my mind, until I can figure out who and what I can trust. What is the reality of my situation?

She places her hands on my cheeks, pulling my face close to pacify me.

"Calm down. Look, it's me. I'm on your side here."

The connection we had felt earlier holds reality together. Although she had withheld information, for some reason, in my gut I feel I can still trust Jessa.

"Alright, I'm just a little spun right now. It's a lot to take in."

She pecks me on the lips and jumps up towards the living room.

"You brought the key with you, right?" She yells from the living room.

It takes me a second to grasp the question. All I can utter are three lousy words.

"Right jacket pocket."

"It's time. We gotta do this quick," she says, rushing back into the room. "If you don't enter The Provax Zone now and head towards The Land of Nod, we will miss our opportunity."

"Can you just cool it and give me a second to wrap my head around this shit? It's not every day I have unintentional Nazi sex and then have to raid a club undercover."

She wraps her arms around me and looks me gently in the eyes.

"We have to do this now. Buckle up, champ."

Although I can't say why, I believe her.

I lift my leather belt off the floor and secure it tightly around my arm. The bone syringe is thick, its needle calcified and rigid. I had used veterinary syringes before that were about the same gauge when the pharmacies started cutting junkies off a few years back, but this looks like it is a whole 'nother beast. The last thing I want is my vein to blow, I proceed with caution.

As my veins rise to the surface, I slide it in carefully. My arm stings with pain. This bitch has got more bite then most. It scrapes against the lining of my vein walls, tearing the skin along with it. I have to be very careful not to stick the needle through the back of the vein into my muscle. I can't afford a miss, and I've only got one shot at this. I pull back and, much to my surprise, the blood doesn't enter the syringe normally. The liquid inside reacts to the blood, pulling it to the center and separating it from the other two liquids that float inside.

As I hold the belt and syringe steady, I look Jessa in the eyes. I push past all the fear of what is to come next and I squeeze out a tight nod of my head in Jessa's direction, signaling her to go ahead and push it in. The plunger clicks and scratches as every milliliter of liquid leaves the syringe and enters my bloodstream.

My pupils pin. Curtains fall. Fade to black.

9 | Lord

The following document was dictated to me on the night of July the Ninth. I wrote it down as the reality was transmuted to me from the High Order. It is not my intent to create a doctrine, for doctrine is the mind-killer. Anything written in words is flawed in describing totality, for the reality we live in is a fluid one. So take note that the following text is only a myth, not a myth in the sense that it is untrue, as the word is commonly misused. Myth as a tool, a tool to practically communicate eternal truths that straight forward words could never possibly hope to communicate. All who read these words have the responsibility to use their experiences in this world to interpret the deeper reality hidden in the words that follow. Unlike any doctrine, this will not solidify your mind with thinking it claims to be definite truth. Instead, it will plant a seed that will grow naturally, as all true life grows.

VII–IX:

The High Order, it is all, it is the essence of being which permeates all realities, both those we can comprehend and those we cannot. It is without beginning and without end and without division or separation.

It is the Word of Man that creates all.

Everything Living and Dead.

Everything Material and Immaterial.

Everything Good and Evil.

The Word of Man lives in paradox and creates polarity.

For how can The High Order commit acts of malevolence against Itself?

The Word of Man infinitely separates The High Order.

Creating Deities who dance endlessly, Deities influencing the very ones who created them.

Our interaction has brought about the Blessing and Curse of Personal Consciousness at the loss of Total Consciousness.

Total Consciousness is only once again possible at the time of The Dissipation

The Dissipation in turn brings the loss of Personal Consciousness, for only when we let our Personal Consciousness go can we be truly conscious of all.

Each of us is a combination of Deities interacting in our minds; the Deities that dance inside us determine who we are.

When our connection lessens, we become Beast.

We are both Instruments and Seers; every creative thought is divine in nature and the revelation of a certain Deity.

Through communion with, and sacrifice to, these Deities, we can change our person, but we must remember that by law, all change has an equal reaction elsewhere, whether on our plane or another, for The High Order is constant.

All communions with Deities are sacrifice, and if one takes on the entire nature of a Deity, they experience The Dissipation, a full sacrifice of themselves.

With constant communion with certain malevolent Deities, one's mind loses a sense of who they are. They start to adapt and morph, and when communion ceases, the process by which a body and mind gain back their natural stasis is the very definition of agony.

All Deities are benevolent, malevolent, or neutral in nature; but do not be fooled. These Deities never have full control over a person; they only exert high levels of influence.

Lady Chance will present Herself to you, but Her lies are but an illusion. There are causalities on so many different levels unseen to us. Only through communion with specific deities are these levels seen.

Never take words at face value. These words especially. Experience is the only and final truth. Only when one brings to an experience the knowledge that is needed can it deeply and fully be understood.

10 | Golden Era Thinking

Everyone is dead and I'm going to live forever.

The Doc says he's working on a cure for The Sickness. He's based his research on the male sexual refractory period. After erect cocks spurt, men's minds have a clarity, a satisfaction, a disgust. He says by modifying the chemicals oxytocin and prolactin, which are the cause for this strange phenomena in the male sex drive, he can rework it to end the drive for junk. The addict will finally feel fully satisfied after one high. A pipe dream I say. An altering of the peripheral autonomic feedback mechanism will change the fine autonomic signals sent to the part of the brain that craves, effectively creating a negative feedback loop. Can a negative feedback loop free us from the stratus of samsara? I'm running low on veins. Abscesses ooze dull pain and spurt heavy puss.

My back cracks and arches in the twenty eighth year of my life. Sitting dejected and alone, haunted by what went wrong and what didn't go right. Forced to commune with simple minded sober addicts. Lust the only thing boiling in their brains. I'm a stranger to this city, but still it lacks novelty. It rings sterile, lips dry. Artificial uniqueness, rebranded hipster culture. Articles of my outward expressions lay strewn across my room, perfectly reflecting my mental status. Shirts crusted with week old jissom lay open beside my bed, representing the sole mental release I have left.

We thought truth to be a lingering mystery that would solve all mankind's problems, but now we swim in more truth than ever thought possible, but for some reason, we prefer the warm shore of ignorance.

"I want to be sober." I'm not even sure if I believe it myself, but part of me hopes its true, and it's the only choice I have left. Nihilism herds me back to the needle. Then the needle has me gasping for air. Rinse and repeat. I've lost count how many times. Hope dissipates. Doom settles.

Romanticization, the art of delusion. We paint over lingering memories and stark reality as we please.

The reasons don't matter. If I can't be with her, then I must block her existence from my brain. It's harder some times than others. Some days it's impossible. Contact would be torture. Bed sweat soaked, memories roll like an unending reel of film. Insomnia wins the night.

Love is fierce, love lost even more so.

We drive in the twilight of our dance, orange sunshine fading in the distance. I can't stand the daylight. I pursue the dreamland of the night in frantic anticipation. Revelation melts on our tongues, bugged up, in love. Mobile fellatio. Her eyes, her smile, her laugh. Never have I seen anything as beautiful as her essence. We lay in the grit of the sand, body in body. Sufjan tinnily steams out of the tiny speakers of my cell phone, but he sounds more pronounced and beautiful in that moment than ever before. Ships fall out of view as they leave port. Waves crash, the moon revealing only what needs to be seen. Hours pass like minutes, every moment brimming with freshness and awe.

My mind throbs in anticipation. The scene a tattered drug minded apartment, friendly territory. Mia runs an errand, time crippled by my detachment. My audio detection pierces the distance. Every car engine and stray step brings hope and disappointment. She enters with ripeness. I fail to bridle the brimming energy. Springing forward I demand her lips. Our bodies conspire. Love, my insufferable master.

The air is of another caliber on the coast. Blown in by the sea, crisp and pure. The air breathes freedom. My ego thrives in the environment, free to be the man I want to be. Parental influence castrated by distance. It is a criminal wonderland and I flourish. Making connections, always on the social game. Schooling quickly becomes a distant second to adventure. Diving deep into an underground few get to experience. Shows and festivals, parties and after-parties are the jungle, drugs are the watering hole. The scene was deep and heavy, how could I deny myself what I had only read about in books. The hippie age is alive and well, and I am ripping right through the heart of it.

Control is shattered, driven by instinct. Roaches burn out. I never wanted to hurt anybody. My first lie, trying to keep all egos in check. Backfire, lost trust, purity shattered. Warm tears. Lost and disconnected. My legs are gone and we will never walk again.

We wake up sick, Mia is rolling on the bed. Wails of pain reverberate off broken walls. She screams for me to fix her, part of me knows in this moment she resents me for the sickness. Blames me. My mind reels. I phone my mother for the fifth time this week, I put on a healthy voice, make up another story hoping to secure enough money to get high. There is an impatience in my voice, I know that she can sense it. I have to keep up the show, I can't push it. No go. I call up Johnny, knowing that whatever plan he has will always have a cost, but I have no other choice. I drive, Johnny steals. We score, we shoot. Johnny steals half my dope and I continue to act like I don't notice. Life again is the greatest gift, and we go on ignoring the mental and physical anguish we woke up to the past five days, and the risks we had to take to fix it. Because once we are high it is all worth it.

Mia returned, I have no idea why. She somehow managed to kick the junk, all the while I progress into madness. I convinced her to pawn her phone for a couple of bags each, it was a good afternoon.

She doesn't want me going around her friends, doesn't trust me. I'm convinced I'm trustworthy but obviously I don't know myself.

We are hanging with some old friends, Mia finally gave in. It felt like old times, not an evil thought in my mind. 'Til they left. I couldn't see the items that filled the room, only their values and ease of theft. Why would they leave me alone in here? My empty wallet screams and the clock that counts down 'til I am sick again ticks with ferocity. They wouldn't miss these text books, I doubt they even need them. I've got plenty of time until they get back. I run them out to Mia's car, the books obviously hidden under my shirt, and I secure them in my bag under the seat.

Upon return they act as if everything's cool but I can tell the energy in the room has changed. The words leave their lips without warning and confirm my fears. They were only a few apartments away and saw it all. Mia begs me to explain. Her face painted heavy with confusion. A shred of hope keeping her emotions from breaking through a dam of deep betrayal. I confess. The dam breaks, tears flood.

I beg him to punch me. I am a worm. He won't grant even my lowest wish.

I hand over my phone, drop her keys on the coffee table and head out the door.

Cars buzz past, none slowing to heed my outstretched thumb. Suicidal thoughts flood my head and I'm not completely sure if i've come to this conclusion as a way to get Mia's attention or if in this moment I truly want to die. I walk towards my death and time stretches on towards infinity.

It's been almost four years since I last saw her. I feel like I am drowning in existential dread and loneliness. My body physically vibrates with these emotions, unable to distinguish emotional pain from physical. I gasp for air, unable to breath, my gasps turn into a choking cry. Tears stream down my face as I'm unable to physically contain these emotions. I just want to be held and I have no one to hold me.

Depression enters my mind as I realize I'd have to pay someone just to be touched in a sensual way. My mind can't comprehend how I could love and live with someone for over two years and then be ripped away as if it never happened. I resent my mother and my family for their negative view of my love and restricting me from seeing her again under the guise of my safety. How could I be that close to another human being and act like it never happened, and be expected to just move on with my life? The tears dry up and I start to panic as I try to remember what it was like. The fact that I'm starting to forget what love was beyond a vague generality is like a knife to the gut. Like a shattered mirror, bits and pieces reflect through my mind, slicing my brain with their sharp edges, but it's starting to feel like a dream I awoke from and can't return to. Slipping away against my wishes as a new day fills my view. All I want is to go back. All I want is to hold my girl in my arms again.

11 | East of Eden

I come back to the present in a room disassociated from memory. Left to molder in a cocoon of my own making, my mind and body crack free from a metamorphosis. As I break from my disorientation, sounds drop into their places. A hairdryer blares from the bathroom in front of me, drowning out the singing of a voice. Whose voice it was, I have no idea.

Blips of a parallel life still echo in my head from the dream state I had just awoken from.

"Come back..." They say. "Come back."

I can smell the rain. The clouds keep even a single ray of moonlight from entering the apartment, leaving me with the soft orange buzz of the streetlights slowly phasing through the window. The hairdryer cuts off and I roll over to see Jessa wrapped in a soft linen towel. I smile and she smiles back. She drops her towel and bounces over to the dresser; carrying herself with the poise of one completely at home in their own skin. She wears nothing so well. She slips on a gothy little black dress that traces her body with such radiance, it seems as if the dress is wearing her.

"You better get ready, we gotta head out soon. We have a limited time before the drug wears off."

She bends over and rails another line of H.

"How was it?"

"Peculiar."

"Always is. You want another hit before we go?" She says.

"Of course."

She carries the mirror over to the bed and kisses me on the forehead as I lean down to take the hit.

I sniff and snap my head back up, taking her lips as if they have an expiration.

"God, this is a strange combo. It almost reminds me of Dexxing. How you are familiar with your surroundings but they just feel... different. Like you are in an alternate universe," I say as I trace my fingers playfully down her hair.

"Can't say I know what you mean. I've never tripped DXM. Always stuck to the traditional shit, LSD, shrooms, and the like."

I smile, always giddy to introduce someone to a drug for the first time.

"That is something we have to fix. By the way, can I hop in your shower? I still reek of sex."

She smiles as she walks pasts, gently bites my ear and whispers, "I'm a fan. It's like I've left my mark."

"God, you're amazing. Alright, where's my bag? Let's get this show on the road."

I throw on some tattered black jeans, an old Cure t-shirt, and my old bomber jacket. I run my fingers through my greasy hair and we head out the door.

We walk arm in arm down the city streets, Jessa slightly leading the way. Her heals click along the sidewalk with purpose, unswerving for the puddles littered along the path. The rain falls so gentle that it appears as if a light fog. Taking a backseat to the action feels good for once. We turn down a back alley, and at the far end, a broad-shouldered man in a suit stands outside a single door, lit an ominous red by the light that hangs above him.

Without warning, Jessa forces me backwards into an alcove in the ally. The cement squeezing between the bricks juts into the back of my head as she violently starts making out with me and stroking my shaft at the same time. She quickly moves down, unzips my jeans, and removes my cock.

"Not that it's not appreciated, but do you think this is the time for this?" I say, regretting it instantly.

"I need you to cum down my throat."

"What?"

"The bone syringe, while active it's sexually transmitted through semen, the only way I'm going to get into this club with you is if you cum down my throat."

"Fuck, okay, this is information you could have told me on the walk over here, but be my guest."

The unexpected nature of the blowjob has me hard instantly. Sucking me off with ferocity, she gets me off in under a minute. She licks her lips, gets up and kisses me, leaving me to zip up.

"Thanks," I say with a hint of sarcasm as I taste my own cum on her tongue.

"Alright, let's go."

"Just like that, huh? God, you are a strange and wonderful woman."

She grabs me by the hand and we make our way down to the bouncer. Jessa exposes the crook of her arm to him and signals to me to do the same. I pull off the left sleeve of my jacket and let it hang down my back. The bouncer unhooks a ultraviolet light off his belt and shines it down Jessa's arm. Her veins separate from her arm in the light and I have to squint to make sure I'm not seeing things. I try to keep my cool as I see what look to be tiny insects poking and prodding along the walls of Jessa's veins. A fear comes over me as I'm not sure if I can handle the same sight in my own arm. He shines the light on me and a sharp pain shoots down my veins as the bugs react negatively to the light, scraping at my vein lining, trying to get out. I grab my arm and wince, trying not to look like a pussy after Jessa barely reacted at all.

"You guys are all good. Enjoy yourselves."

"Oh, we will. Thanks."

Jessa says this as if the bouncer routinely checked for wristbands, pulling me inside with embarrassment.

Somewhat stunned, I stumble inside behind her.

As if in a flash, I find myself thinking about what had led me to this point in my life. Incomplete pictures of childhood bubble up to the surface of my mind. The memory that comes to mind is an early one: my sister, father, mother and I all out on a weekend adventure. Exploring Amish country on a beautiful autumn day, enjoying each other's company and excited to see what our parents had planned next. I vaguely remember an ignorant joy and innocence that had been lost somewhere along the way. I didn't know yet who I was and who I was to become, but I knew that I was loved, cared for, and protected, and in my youth that was enough. My mind traces the memories forward to the present. Passing all the moments things started to break, feeling like a passenger unable to steer a train, heading in the wrong direction.

I remember the moment I lost my faith in God.

The moment my views no longer aligned with my family's.

The moment I felt I had to wear a mask just to fit in any longer.

The moment of my father's death.

The moment I realized I couldn't rely on my family for an honest assessment of the world.

It was as if entering the club triggered a playlist in my mind, a greatest hits, as it were. I come back to the present and realize Jessa is just as stunned as I am.

"Rick... isn't it just a dream?" Her words are soft and wondrous.

I speak, but I can't place where from.

"Ever have a moment of such profound sadness, be it a memory or grief, that as it tried to pass in your mind, you clung tight, deciding rather than to let it drift into the ether of your mind, you'd rather sit in the feeling, knowing that even while bitter the feeling represented something so real that just a taste made you feel alive in a way that you hadn't experience in a long time."

She turns around and cups my cheek.

"I fully understand what you are saying, but Rick, this is not the time. This place is going to play games with your mind, the unbridled flames of your passions will kick up. You've got to use the light within to control that. You have to focus here more than ever."

"It's just... Have you ever been hit with a smell and feel vividly that you are in another time and place? It's as if all the smells from my past wash through this bar, lost... Wandering..."

I kick the emotions and memories away, coming to a realization of the odd fact that I had no reason to be feeling them. I grasp Jessa's hand and follow her inside.

The music in the place had a way of making you feel like you were in an old Italian horror movie. Not a face in the joint was distinctive, nothing stood out, yet it all was egregious to my eyes. Aging white men with graying hair, all sporting different shades of the same Brioni suit. Emaciated young girls hang off each of their arms, ribs visibly poking through their dresses, each of them showing only remnants of their former beauty. I wonder how many of them had to swallow old jizz to get in this place. I notice one of said girls, clearly overdosing, being carted quickly into the back. No one else seems to notice or care.

Jessa and I stick out like sore thumbs, but we make our way to the bar and signal the bartender for a drink. The place had a way of feeling like it was the only place in space and time, stuck somewhere between here and heaven, although hell seemed more likely.

"You guys need a menu?" He asks.

"Yeah, that would be great," Jessa says with a flirty smile.

I take a look at the menu and realize what I'm seeing. There is your typical craft cocktails and beers, but below that is something I thought I would never see in my lifetime.

THE LAND OF NOD

COCKTAILS:

Manhattan

Old Fashioned

Hemingway Daiquiri

Martini Clasico

Sazarac

FROM THE POPPY:

Afghani Heroin #4

Cambodian Black Tar

Opium Classic

OUT OF BODY:

Ketamine

SPECIALE:

Calvin Klein

"Jessa are you seeing this shit? What the fuck is a Calvin Klein."

"Oh you gotta try one, its a line of Ketamine cut with Coke."

I audibly laugh at the creativity of the name.

"I love this fucked up world."

The song changes. The shift in tone is stark. The music is slow and haunting and beautiful. It stikes me as sharply as an alarm to wake up, making me feel the need to suddenly question the reality of things around me, while at the same time lulling me into what felt like a waking sleep. My muscles floated at ease.

Before Jessa can reply, I hear my name bellowed through the bar, which instantly reverses my comfort. The voice rings through the bar a few more times in succession and my mind catches up with itself. I know all too well who it is, and nothing in me wants to face her right now, but I know there is no escaping the situation.

I look back and lock eyes with Zo who is displaying more excitement than is deserved after how things ended between us. What she was doing in this joint I had no clue. She was clearly high. I knew that much.

I could feel the crossing of emotions in my gaze and I wondered if it was as noticeable to the two ladies I found myself between as it was to me. Zo sits perked up in a corner booth, her incandescent brown eyes project a stunning paradox. Her forest black hair cascades down her soft face, and Jesus Christ, does she know how to sex up a dress.

"Who's that?" Jessa asks.

"A past lover," I say, matter-of-fact. "God dammit... Barkeep, load up two shots of that Afghani. We will be in the booth in the corner."

As I get up, it hits me like a glass of water to the face: another scent, much stronger than before, and along with it, a vivid transportation to the memory in question.

Another night with Zo, her hiking up and down the shiny reflective pavement, commanding a condemning tone into her phone. Another phone call shirking the blame onto her man as I wait in the shadows for her to have judged him enough for him to admit guilt and hang up. I do feel a bit guilty, knowing how it feels to be the loser in this situation, knowing you are being lied to but without the power in the relationship to do anything about it. I only hope this doesn't sour her mood for the rest of the night, which feels inherently selfish, knowing the pain being dealt with every word of her conversation.

Ultimately I know I've won, another night where this woman I admire recognizes my value over the man she's comfortable with, but with every action displays dissonance.

She says she feels like she's in a costume in her stiletto heels and knee high socks, but it fits her damn well, and I know she gets off on the power and attention. As much as I love and respect when she

111

wears styles more true to herself, like her military jacket and bandana, it's almost like sighting a rare bird to see her beauty displayed like this.

The lights above buzz and the wind bellows gently, the perfect touch to a perfect night. Just one of many women lost wandering the parking lots of this New Years Eve; caught explaining away their actions to their man. Ultimately choosing the pursuit of hedonism and pleasure and living for their will rather than the will of their man. Knowing their choice to be with me, or others like me, will afford more fun than a night spent with him. Guilty at heart but proud in will.

And just like that, I'm back in the bar, feeling as if I need to shake off the remnants of my past.

I navigate through the crowd and Jessa tags close behind. Taking a seat I restlessly eye the joint for the tray I ordered.

"When did you get into town? Who's this?" Zo says dropping any interest in the first question as soon as Jessa squeezes in beside me.

I catch a clear sense of disappointment and jealously deeply rooted in Zo's face and tone.

"I'm not sure really. Sometimes life leads you places you don't want to be. You should know that better than anyone. The question is what are you doing here?"

I feel my bitterness leaking through my carefully crafted facade and I don't like it. Isn't good for business.

I try to block out the mental imagery of what Zo had to do in order to get into this joint, and how much responsibility I hold in leading her to this point in her life. She doesn't afford me that luxury.

"It's the only place with decent skag in this town anymore. Since you left I've had to learn how to fend for myself, ya know?" She responds with a hint of resentment.

Jessa's phone lights up, and she proceeds to lean over and whispers in my ear the details of the meet. I've always hated the anxiety that comes with an anonymous appointment. It fills me with a strange sense of duty and vulnerability. Jessa gives me a look that implies she doesn't think it's smart to be conducting this business in front of Zo, and since thinking badly of any of my past lovers somehow challenges my own ego, I continue to discuss the matter at hand at full volume in an impudent display of dominance.

"So what are we meeting this Dr. Lee guy for anyways?" I ask.

"Something about a manuscript, I'm really not sure. I just get my orders and I follow them," Jessa says hesitantly.

"Well, let's get high while we wait, shall we? Where is that barkeep? Zo did you want anything?"

"I've already got something on the way, but thanks."

I scan the crowd like a dog impatiently awaiting feeding time. There seems to be an eerie lack of staff in this establishment, but before I can turn around and make a snide comment a server is already here placing an inlaid bronze tray down onto the table. A tray containing three doses and a variety of methods of administration. Zo and I both reach for a rig without hesitation, while Jessa cuts up a small line on the mirror square provided. I display my obvious discontent with Jessa's choice.

"What? We have business to attend to, someone has to be the professional here," Jessa says.

I ignore her obvious snipe and prepare my shot. Before I can even filter it into my rig, Zo has already gotten the needle in and out of her arm. It couldn't have been half a year ago that she couldn't even hit herself and I was a necessary part of that process, which, I have to admit, makes me feel obsolete, while at the same time causing guilt to creep over me in response to how quickly Zo had been caught up in the game. But all that quickly dissipates the moment I push in the plunger.

"God, it's crazy, isn't it?" I mumble as my pupils tighten.

"What's crazy?" Jessa asks.

"The world, this life we find ourselves living. Finding myself here with you two ladies, life just smacks you with the surreal sometimes. Have you ever just taken a moment to think about it? Who would have thought I'd ever find myself in this situation with you two? Man, all the lives that have come and gone on this little blue planet of ours. How many have influenced us, left their imprint, how many more who have left no imprint at all? I sometimes think about what kind of imprint I will leave, or if it even matters to leave an imprint, because how long will it be before no one remembers me at all? I mean, in the grand scheme of things, at the end of it all, there will be no one to remember anything anyways, so why does it matter? Jesus, this is good shit."

I take a second to look around for anyone who might be my man, now seemingly more aware of my task at hand due to my impaired abilities, then I continue.

"I think it's that final thought that makes it so easy for me to live life how I do, why I continue to enjoy the pleasures brought by corrupting my soul, and in turn corrupting the souls of others."

I look at Zo, knowing that last statement applied to her more than anyone. I can't be sure if she was even aware enough after that shot to have taken in what I had said.

"Zo, how many times did you save my life by fucking me?"

The question gets her attention.

"Do handjobs count?"

"Sure, why not?"

"Then two, I guess. There was the time I gave you the handjob in the car on the way to central city, our dealer in the back seat if I remember correctly."

I belly laugh.

"Yes, you're right!"

"And then there was the time I just rode you in bed to keep you from slipping into the beyond."

"Good times."

"Not for me."

The truth stings.

She struggles to open her eyes. The Afghani is intense enough with my tolerance, I couldn't imagine what kind of ether of bliss she must be flying through.

Zo returns to the previous topic.

"Everyone must take responsibility for their own choices in life, right?"

"Yeah, I guess you are right, but can nothing be said of influence?"

"Jesus, Rick. Cut the pontification, will ya?" Jessa cuts in.

"Get used to it." Zo says with a chuckle. "And Rick, as far as influence is concerned, don't give yourself so much credit."

I smirk at her quip and then notice out of the corner of my eye a figure walking towards our booth. I signal the barkeep to clear our tray and bring over a round of drinks.

"All I know is that life is one hundred times more bearable when in love. Reality slips away and you get to write your own story with your partner. Both are slaves on a ship named delusion. If anything, love is the most nihilistic philosophy there is. A true disavowal of any form of truth." I say.

Zo rolls her eyes and Jessa seems stuck with the fact that although her gut disagrees she can't find any fault in what I've just said.

"Rick Thompson?" The man asks as he hovers over the booth. I quickly look at Jessa for confirmation and she nods.

"Dr. Lee!" I say as I shake his hand. "What are you drinking?"

"Only business."

He seems to have a shaky grasp of English, either that or he is a man of few words, and although I trust my connection, it's always hard for me to trust any man not willing to break bread at a business transaction.

I introduce Jessa as my connection in the city. It's harder to explain why Zo is there, but at this point, she is basically asleep, and I'm sure her sex appeal doesn't hurt the situation either.

Our aged rum finally arrives. I take a sip and light a cigarette to compliment the heroin. My tongue grows heavy. I could tell my nodding was annoying the man and annoying Jessa even more so. I push aside the rum and order a black coffee, hoping the caffeine will counteract the effects of the H so I can continue with business.

"Fair enough, onto business then?"

Jessa seems to be getting impatient. She interjects.

"So I'm curious, what makes this manuscript worth 5k?

He pushes the manuscript across the table as if to rid himself of it.

"Well it's yours now. You paid for it, so it doesn't really matter anymore if it's worth the money or not. It's not my job to make you feel good about it, that's up to you to decide. My only job is to make sure you receive it, and I'd say this is a job well done."

I'm at once surprised by his eloquence and taken aback by his bitter attitude.

He shifts his attention back to me.

"I hope you find what you are looking for, Mr. Thompson."

He shakes my hand and proceeds to leave as quickly as he had arrived.

12 | Not The Records!

I awake the next morning in a pool of my own sweat, pockets empty, but happy to find my bed isn't.

I turn to Jessa, who sleeps in peaceful ignorance of the sickness that is taking over my body, and I lay a kiss on her bare arm.

Her skin is soft and brings me a sense of joy despite the panic of withdrawal that is filling my brain.

Then I flow into the greater desires of lesser importance. My nicotine, where is my god damn nicotine, and why isn't it in my lungs and flowing happily through my blood stream?

The good months have passed. You only get five or six once you come back for more, quickly finding yourself in a situation worse than any previous. Jessa doesn't understand as the sickness hasn't caught up to her yet, although I know that if we are to continue at the rate we are going she doesn't have much more than a month of innocence left.

I grab my pack of smokes and sigh heavily at the lack of weight. I dump the last cigarette onto my lap and fumble for my lighter while the night's events start flowing back into my consciousness.

We had spent the last of our money at the club the night before. The junkie in me rarely takes my future situations into consideration. My body aches and my mind is flooded with an overwhelming sense of anxiety. I have no energy, yet I can't sit still. My legs kick, my mind races, and I try to scheme up ways to come up with some money in a city I have little relation to anymore. I start weighing my current moral boundaries against how badly I want to rid myself of this sickness. I shake Jessa awake.

"Hey babe, I'm bad off. We've got to do something. Can you think of anything?"

I am struck with a strange sense of deja vu. Maybe it's because I had just seen Zo the night before, but I know I must have said the same thing, in the same bed, in the same gory situation to Zo in the past. My life feels like a broken record.

My mind follows the memories.

"Maybe we could sell my records?" Zo says with a halfhearted lack of enthusiasm.

I can tell she is growing tired of this morning routine.

I know the records won't sell for nearly enough to get even one dose, let alone one for each of us. I start to get frustrated as I look around the room for other things I might be able to convince her to sell, or at the very least, pawn and buy back. Even though, we both know the day will never come when money not designated solely for more dope is in hand, we mutually agree to believe the lie.

With withdrawal comes a state of emotional rawness and sensitivity. I start to feel guilt as I look around and realize that I've convinced her to pawn pretty much everything of value she had ever owned.

I collapse in defeat and pick up my phone, shooting off a few texts hoping that maybe one of my dealers would be well off enough to give me a front. Even though I set the phone down for a while, it never truly leaves my mind as I anxiously will it to buzz. I begin to ponder on the situation we find ourselves in, and if I was completely responsible.

My thoughts snap forth, back to the night Zo and I were fated to meet, before the chaos and destruction.

I don't even recall finding her that special the first time I had laid eyes on her. Sure I saw a pretty face and a nice body, but there was no attraction in that raw animal center of my brain. I saw it as more than possible that my mind immediately categorized her as unattainable thus not even worth fantasizing about.

But the more I talked to her, the more attractive she became. She always appeared to be fully present and this was the first time since high school where intellect and pure personality consciously changed my sexual attraction towards a person. Sapiosexuality is what they call it, a deep sexual attraction to a persons mind. The prospect of this happening again was exciting, and unbelievably, she came onto me. The feeding of my ego swelled my sexual attraction towards her. It's as if the wall of distraction inherent in my belief that she was out of my league crashed way the moment she asked me out.

Simply put, she made me smile, and I found I didn't smile often unless I was turning darkness into humor, mocking the absurdity of the universe. It seemed like it had been an eternity since I was truly happy. Not just having a good time by shoving drugs up my veins, but truly happy. I was bad off in a bad way. Love was the word that kept popping into my mind, and I knew it was fucking early to say that, but it was my reality. Cynics would classify it as infatuation, but I was well aware of what was gestating inside my chest.

But there was the rub: in her own words, her heart belonged to another. She told me she was in an open relationship, whatever the fuck that meant. It was a bittersweet reality. But god, oh god, those moments. Moments with her qualified as divine. A girl whose presence made me feel comfortable in my own skin.

She invited me back to her place that first night, her book shelves filled with the names of my favorite authors, beautiful art covered the walls of her room. How does a man ignore the talk of fate in moments like these? She pranced around on the bed for me in her designer panties and knee high black socks. Sexual pressure dissolved and all thoughts of either cumming too soon or not even being able to get it up at all left my mind as we gave ourselves over to each other's bodies.

She was a woman who wanted her orgasm and wasn't afraid to tell me how to achieve it, and in that moment I couldn't have cared less. All I desired was to see her face awash with ecstasy.

We held each other, exploring each other's bodies with hands tracing down foreign skin. We took in each other's vulnerabilities with naked eyes. We went back and forth verbalizing compliments, which I'm sure was a mutually pleasing experience. But the night ended as all nights must, and even though she told me that night she was taken, I felt in my heart we were destined to be together.

I was right, but what I was unable to see was the path we were on. I suppose we were always meant to be but travelers on a rocket flown one to many times, flying fast and bright, but exploding under the pressure of our ascent. It left us in nothing but a state of utter deliquescence, our wreckage cratering the ground around us.

13 | The Soul Don't Shine

I find myself lost on the wrong side of paradise.

A look of pity gleams in Jessa's eyes, but she's well aware there is nothing she can do to help me. She suggests I go get some help, she says she has a friend down in Dunsmere who I could stay with, get clean.

Dunsmere is a smaller mainland city, where no one of prominence is birthed.

"Fuck Dunsmere, any city that dies at night is not a city worth living in," I say.

"It would only be for a little while, just to rid you of the sickness."

"I'm not playing this game, and what about the mission at hand? We just received the manuscript. We have work to do."

"Don't start with this again. I don't have time for your games, I'm just trying to help you."

Games? Her words coupled with the panic in my mind start to drive me crazy and anger is my only salve.

"You wanna help me? Find me some god damn money for a shot."

Dope sickness feels like a peg stuck in time's gears. Time goes slower when we are suffering and quicker when we are in moments of joy. It's one of the universe's cruel jokes.

I know deep down that she's right. I can't keep perpetuating this ruse. At the very least, a tolerance break would do me good. I'm not even sure what's driving me any longer. Heroin is a false goal, that when reached, only creates another goal further away. I abide, passively hoping my dreams will be gifted to me. The aspirations to achieve such dreams keep me within a thin shell of hope. Yet I am left to find only utter discontentment upon reaching that goal, realizing that I wasn't living for the dream at all, but it was purely the aspiration that was driving me. A smoker who knows all to well that the craving for another cigarette is always more satisfying than the cigarette itself.

"You can't always use the meaninglessness of the universe to excuse not trying!" She screams.

"I feel like I'm doing a pretty damn good job of it!"

126

I see the pain in her eyes caused by my screaming, and I realize she does genuinely care.

"Alright... I'll fucking do it, but I'm not going to a bullshit rehab or meetings. The moment you admit you have a problem, it defines you in other people's minds. You go to a medical facility and they try and shove a cult from the 1930's down your throat as the cure. Prayer and God, in a medical facility. I'm not having that shit. The level of influence they have over culture and society pisses me off. They are killing people and enslaving them in misery and they don't even know it."

I know how it works, I have seen countless people go through the recovery thresher. It's a classic case of contempt before investigation. They will write the rules, and the rules favor those that write them. They don't hesitate to declare what is right and wrong for the individual, and without even a say in the matter, everyone will adopt the cult's declaration of the individual without question. It devalues and belittles a person. A lack of trust becomes inherent in every interaction. I won't accept judgement for the choices I make. I'm well aware of the level of control I have; I know the things that have strong influence over me. Not many people will judge a man who's eight drinks deep and diving into a bag of cocaine; no friend will dare ask him if that's what he should be doing. Until the moment he admits he has a problem, and then everyone is a moral white knight who can't abide. It's all about perception. Money and success change everything.

If you are poor, you are a junkie nobody. Throw in money and fame and you are a tortured genius.

"Well, maybe you can change things. You always talk about your lack of meaning in your life. Maybe this could be your calling?"

"Jesus, as much as I would love to be the modern day Moses for a bunch of cult-enslaved junkies, I've got my own shit to figure out. Plus, it's not as easy as you make it sound. This would be like trying to take on the Catholic Church. Actually, scratch that, it would be harder then taking on the Catholic Church. I'd not only be taking on multiple 12-step organizations, and their two million members, but the entire rehab system, a thirty five million dollar industry, medical professionals, and ideas that have been propagated into mainstream society through books, films, and music for the past hundred years."

"I don't understand how you can be such a cynic and such a romantic at the same time."

"I'm a living paradox, baby; a bona-fide vessel for the absurdity of life. Besides, in accepting your advice, I am in no way saying I want to live 'clean', whatever that means. But that's whats makes me interesting; no one wants to watch a movie about a character who has it all together"

I really like Jessa. The connection is palpable, but I know my intentions to do this for her aren't entirely driven by love. I know all my motives when trying to be with a woman. Desire for passion, for

128

love, for beauty and connection are all there. But there also exists the desire to influence, to corrupt; desire for others to see what I can "pull off"-- to raise my status in their eyes. And most of all, the desire to be desired. A good woman fuels me more then anything else. My ego swells and a charisma is released that influences all those around me.

I can't say I feel like a good man, although I do have my righteous aspects. But my self awareness regarding the small subsection of my darker motives always leaves me feeling a bit sociopathic; as a white sheet might be ruined by a single stain of blood. But I can't say I ever wanted to be a "good man," my only desire was to be infamous; a man who, through every word and action, confounds the beliefs of society, leaving them unable to explain why they are so drawn to me, despite the fact that I embody everything they are against.

"Look, believe me, babe. There is plenty I want to do in this life, but I gotta do them with style or there is no point," I say.

"And that's exactly what I dig about you," she says with a loving smile. A smile that all but confirms my principles in my mind.

I love her way with words. The beauty in her speech causes me to retreat from my sickness for only a moment, but it is sublime. Beauty in the words of everyday speech is no longer taken seriously. I see this as a falling away of romanticism, a gross cynicism which takes the world at face value. Sadly there is no more time to pretend. Most people are afraid of the vulnerability of sentimentality.

In this moment of physical and emotional weakness, with Jessa by my side, I feel I am finally coming to a place of content acceptance of my existence. We are all actors in a play, acting out a script we wrote ourselves, and nihilism is the realization that no one is watching. But I realize now, that doesn't have to mean we don't enjoy the play, just that we might rewrite a few scenes.

14 | A God Died Today

Although I was depressingly out of money and heroin, I did still have health insurance, so it was off to the doctor to see if I could pull off getting a script.

I take a cold shower to try to cool the sweats, after which I throw on one of my nicer suits. I know playing the game is always important to doctors. All doctors want is for you to give them just enough justification to let them live in their morally gray world.

The streets have a sort of peace to them. I'm out just early enough to beat the business crowd and only a few junkies and street urchins litter the alleyways. The sky projects a bold blue, almost as if nature is mocking me in my present pathetic state.

Visiting the Doc goes as it usually does.

He asks if I'm in pain, I say I am.

"But it's getting better?"

And I say "Yeah, Doc. Like having three fingers chopped off instead of four."

He laughs and writes me a script and I'm out the door in a flash.

The trip to the pharmacy is just as amusing. The Pharmacist is a young, undefined man, who, because of his position, finds the need to bolster himself beyond his means. He tries to empathize with me about my "back pain," quipping that its basically the worst thing in the world.

"Yeah, I agree. The holocaust was pretty overrated. Glad we are on the same page."

He's caught stunned, not sure how to respond. I grab my bag of pills and head back to the house.

Jessa greets me as if she was unaware that time had passed at all. That bitch.

The bottle says to take one every eight hours. I pop four.

She smiles at the sound of the pill bottle, looks up and says

"I'm guessing everything went well?"

"It was a long and tedious process, but yes, we should be straight for the night."

"That sounds like a reason to celebrate. I'll go grab a bottle of wine to help the pills go down easier. A merlot sound alright?"

"Babe, I could be chasing these with toilet water right now and I'd be alright."

"A merlot will do fine then."

Our nightly bottle was always just something cheap and with a label depicting some sort of trendy representation of the criminal or occult. To us, it was the nectar of the gods.

The beautiful sound of the cork popping dissipates time as it occurs exponentially. It wasn't long before the wine was gone and so were our minds. I lay in Jessa's lap, imagining this must be what a dog feels like, simple observations coupled with erratic behavior.

We have somehow become so distracted by our own desires I didn't even take a moment to think about the manuscript 'til now, and in my current state I had no desire to investigate 'til later.

I come to a place of ego softness that allows me to bask in the memories of the past. My mind floats once again to Mia.

I lift the manuscript off of the side table. It feels heavy for the lack of ink on its pages.

I flip it open and all that lays inside are the words "Cure the Desire, Cure the sickness."

I throw the manuscript down in disgust. Jessa is too gone to notice, not that I care to advertise my failure.

But the phrase sticks in my mind.

"Cure the Desire, Cure the Sickness."

"Cure the Desire, Cure the Sickness."

The idea of losing Mia is too much to think about. My body slumps heavy as I try. I realize now that facing the truth was the only way to cure the Sickness. There is no secret fix.

I push forward despite my discomfort. How can a man face losing the one person they felt fate had destined to be with them 'til the end? How can I shake this feeling of universal betrayal?

I knew that it was all absurd, but what a nasty trick for life to play to give me the one thing I desired and not only take it away, but have it ripped away by my own hand.

BY MY OWN HAND.

Images start to appear in front of me.
Gentle at first, like the remnants of a dream, but as I allow them to stay they grow stronger.

The guilt is too much to bear. I start to weep.

I have finally become fully aware of the reality I am living in, no longer feeling the need to push it away for another six hours by shoving a needle up my arm.

Mason didn't kill Mia, I did.

Visions flood my mind fast and quick like an MTV music video.

The powder.

The shot.

The little wince of pain Mia gives me as I pierced her arm.

And how after that, I'd never see a look of pain on that beautiful face ever again.

I took her for granted. I saw her as a cure for my sickness, when in reality I was just transferring vessels.

Jessa wakes up to find me shaking in a pool of my own tears.

I am inconsolable.

Mia changed everything I thought I knew about the universe, and then left me, surrounded by rubble, not even a cornerstone in site.

Where is there for a man to go from there but down? How else can a man rise from that without a deep, self-induced, delusion while putting the pieces back together?

Only the broken man can find hope.

I am lost, but I feel I've won.

It all made sense. Well, what little sense a bad trip could. I realize now that Jessa was just another young girl I was bringing into my madness, and for the first time in a long time a voice inside me cares more about the damage I might do rather than another nihilistic, drug-fueled relationship. Is this to be the end of young girls and young adventures? Only god could say, but the causalities of this predilection are clear now, and I think it's time for me to be on my way.

My intention is never to break souls. That hurts me to think about. I don't want to be thought of as a bullet to be dodged; the heroin is the bullet. I'm just a vessel. The girls choose whether or not they want to open that door. I just hold the key and knew the way. And I'm not saying that I don't enjoy parts of that path, but I won't let it define what I want out of a future relationships, or the fate inherent within those relationships.

15 | I Wouldn't Kill Myself Without Ya.

A God died today and the revelation has left me paralyzed. I lay still, eyes wide, tears flowing down my face, steady and strong, coupled with no physical reaction whatsoever

All I want to do was stay in the safety of my memories.

Relive as long as I could the memories of Mia before they faded away.

I start where everything starts. And all it takes is the smell of a relit cigarette.

Mia and I are outside the town pool hall. I relight the last cigarette that is sitting low in it's pack.

The night is cool and calm, but the instant draw I have towards this girl I now must know roars in subtle bursts.

I try to be flirtatious but my voice cracks.

I slap my face a few times.

"Sorry, machinery must be on the fritz."

She ails me with an amused smile.

The moment seemed to end too soon, and she was gone as quickly as she had jumped into my life. I hoped it wouldn't be the last time.

Three AM the same night, the fates decide to grant that wish. I find myself at Josh's grabbing some cocaine to keep the night going, Zo was in tow.

And Mia, Mia sat there on the couch like a siren beckoning.

Is there anything more wonderful than a confident woman that plays you like a harp?

Pulling you in slowly over time but in such strong bursts that are locked in body and soul. All it takes is a moment of that sultry tone of voice, eye contact separated by nothing but passion, and light contact that couldn't in that moment be bested by even the best of handjobs.

I make sure to get her number, and I leave once again with stars in my eyes, hoping this was just the beginning of the ascent, that I was here for the start of something powerful.

The next day, I find myself a bipolar nightmare, always either filled with a joy my face can't contain or an exhausting level of fear.

I like this girl so god damn much, I can't recall the last time. I don't think there was a last time for a feeling like this. It's so good, so strong, it screams loud in enemy territory.

I am wracked with fear.

The kind of fear you know is irrational, yet you can't shake it. All thats left to do is soak in the glorious suffering. Be glad that I was fortunate enough to receive this beautiful pain.

I'm stuck in a constant state of analysis, hopelessly sorting through the tea leaves thinking I might catch a glimpse of what's to be.

I try to combat the fears with good thoughts, which is a mistake.

Fear Trumps All.

All this does is expose the good thoughts to be infected by the fear.

Only causing the fear to grow stronger.

I feel weak.

Pitiful.

Brought to my knees by the one thing I always dreamed to be.

It's knowing she is everything I want, but am I everything she wants?

I stop by The Temple on the way home and order a cup of black coffee.

It bites just like I need it too.

"How you doing, Rick?" Frank says.

"Terrible."

"What's wrong, my friend?"

"I think I'm in love, and it's not good."

"Tell me about it."

"Her name is Mia. Skin like a warm Autumn day. Brown eyes that swirl like dark coffee. A smile and carefree essence that, when carried by her natural genuineness, both locks you in place and pulls you in at the same time.

I'm telling you, Frank, her beauty belongs trapped in the black and white film stock of a French New Wave picture.

I don't know what to do with myself.

I don't want to ever imagine a day where she's not in my life."

"Yep Rick, sure does sound like you have it bad. How 'bout a little whiskey in that coffee?"

"Sounds good, Frank. Thanks."

The third night, I invite her over to my place.

We make love, a lot, and if we aren't making love then we are holding each other or staring into each other's eyes in utter amazement, shaking our heads in constant disbelief.

Every moment with her felt lifted out of a novel. It was clear at this point we were in love, despite it being a fact unspoken. Night three is a hard night to tell the truth.

But she makes it easier.

We lay on my futon and discuss polyamory and our future. The conversation builds towards the obvious climax, which is when she stops me.

"I want to say something, but I want to hear you say it first."

I rise up onto my knees, stunned. Obviously it was 'I love you.' Every action between the two of us screamed it, and yet I couldn't utter a peep. What if I was wrong?

"Whisper it in my ear," she said.

I leaned slow, taking my time to build up the nerve to follow through with the swing.

The moment played out the only way it could have.

"I love you," I whisper.

She lets out a sound somewhere between a sigh and a moan, kisses me, and leans back with a smile that makes me believe there is nothing to be feared anymore.

"Baby..." She says the word as if she is having trouble getting it out. It roars out in a whisper. Cuts through me like glass. As if her soul were gasping for air.

"I love you so god damn much," I say, feeling like I live, for once, in a state of perfection.

The pipe had burst and the love flowed, and it flowed strong and heavy.

We both break into laughter, knowing the beauty in it all is just too overwhelming.

"You ever just cackle because you feel like you are pulling one over on the man upstairs? What did I do to deserve this?" I say.

"Every moment I'm with you."

"You know the best way this ends is one of us watches the other one die, and I'd choose it over anything else in the world."

"Baby…" She says it again, like a psychic calling card, a safe port in the storm. When I hear her say that, I know everything is all right.

My confidence rose ten fold the next day. I floated a foot off the ground. It only takes one true believer to create a god.

I listened to "Here, There, and Everywhere" by The Beatles on the way to work, seemingly for the first time.

I sent Mia a text message.

"Huh?"

"I just said that loving you makes all those Beatles songs I've heard since I was a kid finally make sense."

I worried I was laying it on a bit to heavy. That's the problem with love, nothing feels heavy. You feel capable of lifting a 10-ton truck and as vulnerable as a child in the same moment.

She hits me like a xanax, not the loss of memory, not the assholery, nor the sleepiness.

But like that shot of sheer will, where you know the clerk is staring at you, but you continue to shove the candy bar in your pocket anyways, while staring right back at him. Dead in the eyes.

We were outliers on the map of love.

Mia spends the night again, after a long day of us each working she passed out the moment I get done giving her head.

She fidgets in her sleep like she was having a vet's nightmare, but that only made me want to hold her tighter. It made me wonder what she could be dreaming to cause such a stir.

What terrible thing could she have in her past that would make me love her even more?

The miraculous makes its descent into normality as it seems to do with time, but only if I didn't take a step back, and I tried every day to find time to really see how miraculous it all was. The change doesn't make it any less special to me. I loved her more every single day. She turned every experience virgin, as if I was born anew.

Who were the men she was with before me? Were they still standing? How could anyone lose her and not their minds?

16 | Good Natured Chaos

A dog barks, and kids can be heard screaming outside. A kind of good natured chaos. Cars whooshing by play the strings of the orchestra, giving a flow to the staccato nature of the rough housing. And then it just stops, leaving me to question if I ever heard it at all. No cars go by, no joyful playing, no dog. Where did they go, and so suddenly? It puts a stark change in perspective on the room around me. I feel more set in place. Suddenly, it's the middle of the night, and I'm in the same chair, staring at the same screen, coming up empty.

The silence gave the rats skuddling through the walls a little more pop than usual.

This was it, this was the moment. I am finally a novelist.

What more proof do you need? I'm stuck here, stricken with insomnia, no words in my head, staring at the blank page.

And now I am plagued by the sound of rats in my walls.

All that's left to do is buy a cat and name him "Nigger Man"

Hp Lovecraft joke.

Poor taste, I know.

I feel more picky than I usually do.

Not just in my writing, although that is true, but in life in general.

More picky with food.

My friends.

How I spend my time.

Surprisingly more picky with women, which hasn't made the loneliness any easier, let me tell ya.

I'm starting to see that all the things that turned me on about women in my twenties, were attributes that lead to frustration, although fuck, were they fun during the good times, and there were a lot of good times.

A lot of bad times too.

But I find they usually balance out over time; either that or just become a little less heavy to bare.

It's been an unassigned goal of my past to bring out the worst in women, and I think it's time now to try my hand at the opposite.

The point is, I know now carrying around someone's emotional weaknesses' just because they get your prick hard every night is not the way to go.

In this moment, I feel somewhat evolved.

Like I've reached one of those rare milestones in my life, an expression of growth, a marker showing I'm headed the right way.

Maybe the american dream has some life in it yet.

It's a relief, actually.

You spend so many years wondering if you will even live to see the next one.

Invested so deeply in your art and your experiences, yet not quite knowing how to balance the two.

Only to find yourself confused in a place of productivity and general contentment.

That's all a man can ask for.

Luckily, he can take a lot more.

Made in USA - Kendallville, IN
1123190_9781094837673
06.12.2020 0743